The truck st
to pick up sp

The chain-covered tarp beat against the back door soundlessly, the noise lost in the grinding of the engine.

Bolan was in full stride, gaining on the vehicle, his legs aching from the effort. Finally he reached out and grabbed the chain, losing his step as the truck shifted into higher gear. He pulled upward, the agony shifting from his legs to his arms. He willed himself to hold the grip, gritting his teeth as his body slapped against the side of the truck.

Corsini's Cadillac whipped around the corner, the beams of its halogens splashing his legs. Bolan saw a muzzle flash erupt from the passenger side, followed by others. Then the truck started zigzagging, as if the driver was trying to shake him off.

As the warrior inched slowly higher, he felt a searing pain along his leg. He missed his handhold and went swinging wildly away from the truck.

MACK BOLAN.

The Executioner

DON PENDLETON'S

THE EXECUTIONER®

FEATURING MACK BOLAN®

WILD CARD

A GOLD EAGLE BOOK FROM

WORLDWIDE.

TORONTO · NEW YORK · LONDON · PARIS
AMSTERDAM · STOCKHOLM · HAMBURG
ATHENS · MILAN · TOKYO · SYDNEY

First edition August 1990

ISBN 0-373-61140-4

Special thanks and acknowledgment to
Mel Odom for his contribution to this work.

Printed in U.S.A.

I rate the skilful tactician above the skilful strategist, especially him who plays the bad cards well.
—Sir A.P. Wavell:
Soldiers and Soldiering, 1939

I intend to employ no new tactics against today's enemy, the drug king. Although he's more ruthless than yesterday's enemy, he's driven by the same motives, and *that* makes him vulnerable.

—Mack Bolan

THE
MACK BOLAN®
LEGEND

Nothing less than a war could have fashioned the destiny of the man called Mack Bolan. Bolan earned the Executioner title in the jungle hell of Vietnam.

But this soldier also wore another name—Sergeant Mercy. He was so tagged because of the compassion he showed to wounded comrades-in-arms and Vietnamese civilians.

Mack Bolan's second tour of duty ended prematurely when he was given emergency leave to return home and bury his family, victims of the Mob. Then he declared a one-man war against the Mafia.

He confronted the Families head-on from coast to coast, and soon a hope of victory began to appear. But Bolan had broken society's every rule. That same society started gunning for this elusive warrior—to no avail.

So Bolan was offered amnesty to work within the system against terrorism. This time, as an employee of Uncle Sam, Bolan became Colonel John Phoenix. With a command center at Stony Man Farm in Virginia, he and his new allies—Able Team and Phoenix Force—waged relentless war on a new adversary: the KGB.

But when his one true love, April Rose, died at the hands of the Soviet terror machine, Bolan severed all ties with Establishment authority.

Now, after a lengthy lone-wolf struggle and much soul-searching, the Executioner has agreed to enter an "arm's-length" alliance with his government once more, reserving the right to pursue personal missions in his Everlasting War.

1

His final recon for the night's maneuver complete, Mack Bolan powered the Corvette around the corner at the red light and took a side street. He switched the radio off as the sports car glided into the alley behind the bar he'd staked out an hour ago, then killed the lights as he parked near a row of battered trash cans. The engine died with a low-throated rumble.

Bolan reached across the seat and checked the handcuffs he'd bolted to the metal framework of the car when he'd purchased it earlier in the afternoon. Then he laid them on top of the seat and covered them with a Miami newspaper he'd bought while waiting for the dealership to service the Corvette. The paper had been filled with reports of a recent flood of Colombian cocaine in the Miami area, but the stories had held less real Intel than he'd gleaned from the streets in the past twelve hours.

Some of the reporters had talked of a drug war in the offing. That was what had brought the Executioner to Miami. A handful of good cops had already been burned, and the stakes were mounting.

If the Intel Bolan had received was on the money, it was going to mount a lot faster and get a lot higher than most of the officials were expecting.

Satisfied with the strength of the cuffs, he clambered out of the car, then took a chopped-down M870 riot gun from the trunk. The trunk light didn't come on, because he'd taken the bulb out after making the purchase.

The riot gun tucked up neatly under the light trench coat he wore.

A balmy wind filled the alley, whipping in from the coast, carrying a further threat of rain. Puddles from the brief downpour earlier had formed on the ground, resembling pools of black ink.

The bar had a back door that led out onto a concrete loading dock for deliveries. Twisted metal pipe railing long overdue for a new coat of paint framed it.

He circled the one-story structure, going over everything he'd noticed during his brief visit that afternoon. It was a biker bar. The big customized choppers lined up in the front parking area testified to that. He glanced at them in passing, making sure the motorcycle he'd been waiting for was still there among the two dozen other bikes he'd counted.

It didn't quite qualify as a hardsite actually. The bikers were big and mean and tough and wouldn't hesitate to kill him once the opening numbers on this gambit had been kicked into play, but Bolan was counting on the suddenness of the takedown to freeze many of them. And the fact that they wouldn't be expecting a brazen move on their home ground.

The bar belonged to the Outlaws, as did most of the prostitution and drug-running in the area. It was one of their legitimate operations, showing a profit every year that seemed improbable, yet not so far over the line as to draw immediate attention. One of Bolan's sources had assured him the motorcycle chapter funneled illegal moneys through the business, but it wasn't one of their prime outlets.

The cut-down M870 riot gun was for effect primarily, and because he could use it to menace a whole room at a time. The Israeli Desert Eagle .44 rode at his right hip, and the

Beretta 93-R was in shoulder leather. The trench coat covered it all and was as dark as the blacksuit he wore under it.

Two windows were inset on either side of the stained, white entrance that had Club Members Only stenciled in streaky blue paint across it. Sandwiched between the dirty panes and the dusty brown curtains were twin neon beer signs. The first half of the one on the left had burned out some time ago and only flickered occasionally. The muffled backbeat of rock music filled the night air within two or three yards of the entrance.

Tightening his hold on the pistol grip of the riot gun, Bolan twisted the doorknob and followed it inside.

The night outside was dark and oppressive with the chance of sudden rain, but the inside of the tavern was murky, permeated with the smells of cigarette smoke and stale sweat, leather and beer, oppressive with restrained violence.

Three naked girls, aged way past their chronological years, gyrated on the shallow stage under bright lights, trying in vain to find some semblance of rhythm with the loud music. The bar occupied the left side of the tavern. Bottles in different sizes, shapes and colors made up a fragile army along the mirrored sections behind the long-haired bartender. Round and square tables filled the floor in front of the bar and the stage area. A quick glance revealed at least thirty men lounging around the tables.

A gradual hush fell over the dancers' unappreciative audience as they realized an outsider was among them.

Bolan could feel the quietness as it spread, could trace its movements through the crowd with the combat senses he'd honed in Vietnam's jungles. It was an animal kind of fear, a wariness that would result in bloodletting if the wrong move was made too suddenly.

The bartender came to laconic attention behind the scarred bar and turned to face Bolan. His sandy hair caught the reflected highlights from the array of bottles behind him, lending him a strange halo effect. His arms were heavily tattooed with a mixture of biker designs and those received in military service, and the gray Miami Hurricanes T-shirt he wore contrasted with the white apron he had around his waist.

Bolan could tell from the bartender's posture that the man kept some type of weapon under the counter. His gaze swept across the room again, searching for the biker his Intel had steered him toward. Skip Cullen managed most of the cocaine outlets operated by the Outlaws in Miami. The newspaper photograph Bolan had seen of the man had been three years old and grainy even before being put on microfiche at the public library. An informant had provided a description of Cullen's Harley, which had a distinctive paint job, and had named the Red Rooster as a favorite hangout for Cullen and his cronies.

After spotting Cullen at one of the tables nearest the dancers, Bolan looked back at the bartender and stepped forward. The bar gave the widest view of the tavern, besides being nearest the rear exit and providing a small amount of cover. It had been designed that way.

"Something I can help you with?" the bartender asked, making no move to lean across the counter.

"I'd like a drink," Bolan said with an easy smile as he relaxed against the counter.

The bartender shook his bangs out of his face. "Got a problem, though, mister. You gotta be a member to get service here. Didn't you see the sign outside?"

"Can't say that I did," Bolan replied. He kept the smile in place.

"Well, there's one out there. This here's a private place. Members only."

Bolan nodded. "I understand that, but I'm just here for a drink and to maybe catch a look at a few girls. Just act like

I'm one of the guys. Hell, I got plenty of money, so you don't have to worry about me stiffing you for the bar tab.''

"I look like a guy who has to worry about that?" The bartender flashed him a crooked grin that held no mirth. "One word from me, and I got a dozen guys in here ready to break your damn arms."

Using his left hand, Bolan tossed a money clip onto the countertop. "Like I said, pal, I got money. All I want is a drink and to watch the girls dance. This ain't my town, and I don't feel like going to one of those fancy joints down on the strip and paying nine prices for a beer."

The bartender's eyes touched on the hundred-dollar bill on the outside of the money roll, then returned to scrutinize Bolan's face.

There was a pregnant pause from the jukebox in the corner as records swapped places, then rock-and-roll thunder refilled the small tavern.

"You don't look like the kind of guy who'd dig this kind of scene," the bartender said.

Bolan shook his head, as though perplexed. "Look, I don't know why you gotta be so hardass about this, pal. I'm just a guy willing to spend a little money, have a good time all by myself and maybe turn over a few memories while I do it. Don't tell me you got it so good you can afford to turn away the business."

The bartender smiled as he looked at the money again, then leaned in closer to the counter. His hidden hand moved forward.

Bolan caught the movement from his peripheral vision.

Some of the background conversation had started up again but it was sporadic and speculative.

Heavy boots with hobnails thumped across the floor toward Bolan's back.

Turning slowly, Bolan kept the bartender in view as he noted the approach of a burly biker.

The man was big, easily dwarfing the Executioner's six feet three inches and almost doubling his body weight. His fiery red beard looked tangled and unkempt. Wraparound sunglasses hid his eyes, and a handkerchief with white polka dots covered his head, channeling a single twist of hair down his back. He came to a stop on Bolan's left and leaned on the bar, smiling like a simpleminded giant. Sour body odor and the smell of oil and gasoline clung to him like an invisible second skin.

"Havin' any problems, Gene?" the big man asked the bartender.

"This guy don't seem to understand this club is private," the bartender said. "Doesn't mind flashing big bucks around, though." He pointed to the money clip.

The biker nodded. "What you doing here, man? You look too damn straight to be interested in a joint like this."

Bolan gave him a salesman's smile. "Comes from living right and this job I got now that turns a lot of this country into a one-night stand for me. I knew a few bikers from when I was in Vietnam, and got invited to church a few times after we got back stateside. I got involved in some riding for a few months while I spent my back pay, then went out and got a job. But every now and then I like to find a place like this and hang out, remember a few of the old lies that got swapped around between members."

"Somehow I can't see you for a groupie, man," the big biker said. He grinned evilly, revealing an expanse of stained bridgework. "Me and a couple of the boys had a bet goin' between ourselves. Maybe you can settle it for us."

Bolan didn't say anything, sensing the tension in the room was welling up. Even the dancers had stopped their gyrations when the big man had approached him.

"Now, Jojo, he had you figured for a faggot. Figured you thought this was a boy's club and was coming in for some rough trade."

A roar of laughter went up from the crowd, for a moment drowning out the rumble coming from the jukebox.

"Now, me," the biker went on, "I got other ideas. I come over here to get a whiff of you myself 'cause I thought I caught a distinct pig odor about you."

Out of the corner of his eye, Bolan saw the bartender relax, obviously satisfied that the big man was going to take care of things. He shifted his balance, readying himself to make his move. The biker had come from Cullen's table, so it was easy to assume Cullen was protecting his own interests. The cocaine pipeline coming through Miami was hot property now, and everyone was scrambling for a piece of the action.

"Maybe you got it figured wrong on both counts," Bolan said, maintaining a disarming and carefree expression.

The biker appeared to think that over for a moment, but Bolan knew the indecision was all part of the big man's act. The guy gnawed on a callused thumb, then leaned toward Bolan and took another deep breath. He rocked back on his heels. "Naw, I don't think so, man. You got a definite pig odor about you." He grinned. "How 'bout it, champ? Are you a cop or a narc? The law says you gotta tell me if I ask."

Bolan loosened his stance, knowing it was time to kick the opening numbers into play. The crowd had relaxed again, satisfied he was no threat because he'd played the mouse for them, watching as the tomcat closed in. "No," he replied, "I'm not a cop."

The biker turned back to the crowd, mimicking a Can You Believe This Shit look on his round face.

Bolan brought the riot gun out from under the trench coat smoothly, continuing a brief arc that caught the biker flush on the jaw. He was moving before the guy could fall backward, and his arm shot across the counter just as the bartender was reaching behind the bar.

The dancers screamed and fled the stage area as vicious oaths erupted from the seated bikers.

The Executioner caught a handful of his quarry's long hair and yanked, reeling the man in. He vaulted the counter and landed on his feet on the other side of the heavy bar, maintaining his hold on the bartender and the riot gun.

"What the hell is goin' on?" someone yelled.

"Somebody shoot the fucker!" another voice ordered.

Something bright and slender flashed in the bartender's hand as he tried to bring it up to point at Bolan.

Kicking out, Bolan knocked the pistol from the man's grip and sent it spinning away. Using his hold on the bartender's hair, he slammed the man's head into the bar and felt the body relax into unconsciousness. Then he turned his attention back to the crowd, sliding down the length of the counter to cut off escape out the rear exit.

Part of the bottle army behind him exploded, sending fragments splashing onto the shattered mirror.

The gunman was standing next to one of the windows, still yanking the trigger as the pistol belched flame and searched for its target.

The Executioner whirled, tracking the riot gun onto the man's midsection, then squeezed the trigger. The resulting explosion from the weapon blew all sound from the inside of the bar for a time as the double-ought buck caught the biker in the chest and slammed him through the window.

Bolan racked the specially modified pump on its shorter than original stroke and chambered another round. Wooden chips stung his face as he squeezed off the shot. The muzzle-flash belched brightly from the barrel of the riot gun as the load caught the next target in the shoulder and spun him around, depositing the guy in a pile of screaming agony.

He pumped the weapon again, knowing there were only three shots left before he had to reload.

One of the bikers had carried in a machine pistol, and the pop-pop-pop of autofire rattled across the ragged line of bottles.

Bolan swung away, locking in on the rapid muzzle-flashes. He fired, racked the slide, then fired again, taking no chances with the automatic weapon inside the small confines of the bar. Even if the man never succeeded in hitting him, he still needed Cullen alive. Both loads of buckshot hit the target, blowing him backward across the room to crash into the wall.

Pumping his weapon, Bolan chambered the final round, knowing the Desert Eagle and Beretta were just a tug away from entering the confrontation.

The rest of the bikers had dropped to the floor, using upended tables and chairs as cover. No one appeared interested in reaching for any more guns.

The big biker stirred and shook his head, then grabbed the bar to bring himself to his feet with a growl of rage.

Bolan let him see the business end of the riot gun. "You're a big target," he warned. "Now sit back down."

The biker sat as the confused look drained from his wide eyes and fear poured in.

"What the hell do you want with us?" someone asked from the floor.

Bolan locked eyes with Cullen, then covered him with the muzzle of the riot gun. "Get up slowly," he ordered.

The biker stared back defiantly. "If you're gonna kill me, get it over with."

"Get up."

Cullen didn't budge.

Bolan pointed the riot gun meaningfully. "I need you alive, Cullen, or I don't need you at all. It's your decision."

Keeping his hands locked behind his head, Cullen forced himself to a standing position. He was tall and lean, with a pronounced widow's peak capping hair that was relatively short when compared to that of the other Outlaws.

Bolan knew from the Intel he'd gathered that Cullen had only recently been released from prison. The man was smart, good with money and with strategies. That was why Cullen had been brought in on the new cocaine outlet that had cut through Miami. Bolan wanted to know who had helped set him into business in the drug empire that was just getting off the ground.

"You're crazy, man," Cullen said. "You ain't gonna get away with this shit. I don't know who you are, but..."

"That's right," Bolan said in a graveyard voice, "you don't know who I am. Now shut up and get over here. Slowly."

Cullen stepped through the tangle of arms and legs sprawled across the floor as grumbling curses followed his movement.

Bolan said, "The instant your hands drop from your head without me telling you to move, I'll shoot you and move on to the next target. Understand?"

Cullen nodded. A sheen of perspiration gleamed on his high forehead.

"We're going out the back door," Bolan told him, "and you keep in mind I'm bringing up the rear. You get any ideas about turning this into a footrace, and it'll be one where you end up dead last. There's a car in the alley. It's unlocked. You get in on the passenger side. Now move."

"You're a dead man," Cullen promised as he walked toward the back door. "You have no idea of the kind of people you're fucking around with."

"Don't worry," Bolan assured him as he trailed him toward the exit, "you're going to get the chance to help enlighten me."

The Executioner kept the riot gun aimed toward the group of bikers as he edged sideways to keep his prisoner in view as well. He could hear small, scrabbling movements the men made, heard the squeak of chairs shifting across the wooden floor. Dozens of sullen eyes followed his movements, and he could sense the collective readiness to kill.

Cullen paused at the doorway, and Bolan spotted the tremor that ran through the man just before the biker whirled suddenly.

Before Cullen could close in on him, the Executioner lifted his leg in a short roundhouse kick that thudded into Cullen's face. The biker flew backward from the impact, striking the door and shattering it from its hinges.

Knowing the controlling balance of the play had suddenly shifted with the possibility of Cullen's escape into the alley, Bolan triggered the final round of the riot gun and exploded two of the lamps hanging over the tables. Glass shards rained down on the bikers as he dropped the riot gun and drew the .44.

Outside, the air was immediately fresher, with more of a chill now.

Cullen was sprawled across the railing that ringed the dock area, caught between the remains of the flimsy door and the ironwork.

Moving in on the man, Bolan blocked an ineffectual blow with his arm and smashed the Desert Eagle against his prisoner's temple. Blood was already running from Cullen's nose and mouth from the kick. Gripping the man's leather jacket, the Executioner hauled the biker to his feet and pushed him down the steps toward the waiting Corvette.

Cullen halted at the bottom of the steps, clinging to the railing and grumbling in a harsh voice. "You're gonna die, asshole, and you're gonna die real slow." He swayed uncertainly, trying to focus his eyes into a worthwhile glare.

Bolan rapped the back of Cullen's head with the .44 as a warning, then forced the man ahead of him. The numbers had run out on this one, he knew, and he was operating on borrowed time. Even if Cullen hadn't been an important cog in the motorcycle gang's cocaine outlet, the bikers inside the tavern would be out for blood anyway. It would have been easier if he didn't need Cullen alive.

Footsteps echoed through the alley as the night came alive with screaming sirens.

"Son of a bitch," Cullen grunted as he was pushed forward again.

A dark shadow peered out of the wrecked back door of the tavern.

Twisting the Desert Eagle from Cullen's back, Bolan snapped a round in the shadow's general vicinity and was instantly rewarded by a yelp of pain.

The shadow went away.

Conscious of the approach of the local law as well as the fact that he could no longer contain the building, Bolan grabbed the back of Cullen's shirt as the man opened the Corvette's door. The interior light didn't come on, either, because he'd removed it along with the trunk light.

"Get in," Bolan ordered, pushing down on his prisoner's head to keep it under the lip of the sports car's low roof. One of the last things he needed to happen was for Cullen to knock himself out and become deadweight. He jerked the handcuffs from under the newspaper as the man sat down. He snapped them into place around the captive's wrists and shut the door.

Running steps echoed with a peculiar ringing cadence as two men came around the side of the tavern. Gunfire tore holes in the asphalt pavement of the alley near Bolan's feet. More shots raked the rear of the Corvette, imploding the back window.

Raising the heavy .44 into target acquisition, the Executioner caught the first man in the chest, and the force of the 240-grain slug tossed him backward. The follow-up round spun the second man around as his feet skidded out from under him.

Throwing himself across the hood of the car, Bolan slid to the other side. The trench coat swirled around him in a dark blur, catching at least one bullet from another biker taking up a stance inside the back door of the tavern, where the shadows provided cover.

Bolan steadied himself behind the bulk of the Corvette, resting his hand and arm across the top of the sports car as he tried to use what little light still issued from the bar to outline the shooter against the darkness. Centering on a muzzle-flash, a silhouette blurred grudgingly into view. Squeezing carefully, he sent three 240-grain slugs deep into the shadows.

The silhouette ripped free of the doorway and stumbled inward to signal a new chorus of profanity and feminine shrieks.

Bolan opened his door and slid behind the wheel, taking the ignition key from where he'd left it under the seat. The big engine rumbled to life at once.

Two shots thudded against the sports car's roof as he stabbed the stick into reverse. Cullen had his head down, trying in vain to cover up with his manacled hands. "You stupid bastard!" the man yelled. "You're going to get us both killed!"

The snatch wasn't going anywhere near as smoothly as Bolan had anticipated. Cullen had more of a backing from the Outlaws than he'd expected. And the police had somehow been too damn close. Still, it was the only game in town, and he'd never turned down a hand he'd been dealt yet. Not as long as the stakes were worth it and he knew the deck wasn't stacked against him. Long odds were more often than not the only odds the Executioner garnered at all.

The tires gave out a banshee scream as they fought for traction when he popped the clutch. He steered with his left hand, resting his right arm and the Desert Eagle on the seat backs.

A man jumped free of the tavern as the Corvette went into reverse. Autofire flamed to life in his hands. Bullets chopped into the sports car's body with hollow thuds.

Before the man could adjust his aim, Bolan twisted the wheel, sending the Corvette into a tight embrace with the brick wall of the tavern. A grating sound issued along the passenger side as the uneven brick surface ripped paint and body moldings from the car.

Bolan fought the wheel, forcing the Corvette to stay with the grind, feeding it power. Trash cans scattered, and the smell of tortured rubber burned through the air. A brief yell ripped through the carnage and was swept away as the shooter went down under the sports car's tires.

The car rocked out onto the street, then skidded in a tight semicircle when Bolan dropped the .44 between his knees, locked the brakes as he tapped the clutch and shifted into first gear.

Hoping he hadn't damaged the sports car's sensitive steering when he ripped it along the tavern wall, Bolan dropped a heavy foot on the accelerator and felt the ass end of the Corvette dancing as it struggled for traction.

Traffic was sparse, and what little there was didn't bother to compete for the street.

Glancing in the rearview mirror, Bolan saw that at least four Miami PD squad cars had roared into the parking lot of the Red Rooster. Bikers had scattered across the motorcycles and were attempting to flee even as the uniformed officers tried to close them in. A squad car slid into position behind the Executioner, locking onto his tail with flashing lights.

Bolan shifted gears, skidding across the first intersection as he built up speed. He didn't want to tangle with the law. Hal Brognola wasn't even aware of this Miami strike. The

Intel had been too sudden to allow the grim warrior's Justice contact to erect any kind of cover, and too damn hot to allow to cool. And if the rumblings Bolan had heard so far were any indication, the federal networks were so leaky on this operation that the pipeline would have known about him before he could have taken this first step against it.

If the police got a hold of him now, there was every chance he would be processed through the system before Brognola even knew he was in trouble. And once Bolan's true name was discovered, it would be too late to do anything.

It was a major drawback he had in his arm's-length relationship with Justice these days, but it was also what allowed him to play a free hand wherever he felt needed. Like now. Like in Miami.

He took the next intersection at the last possible moment as the cruiser crept up on him, barely succeeding in cutting off an eighteen-wheeler taking the downtown circuit. The police car wasn't so lucky. Twisted out of control by the centrifugal force it had built up, the cruiser broadsided the cab of the big truck and effectively blocked the street.

A few streets farther on, he decreased his speed, heading for the beach and a place to dump the car. The ownership papers would lead investigators nowhere, he knew, but it was dangerous to stay with the car now.

So, yeah, the heat was on in Miami.

And the Executioner was going to take an active part to make sure the right people got torched when the lid came off the simmering witch's brew.

2

"So, if you're not a cop," Cullen said, "what are you?"

"An interested party," Bolan responded.

"Yeah, a tough guy, right?" Cullen sneered. He wiped at the dried blood on his face with his manacled hands. "Well, I'll tell you right now, the guys you're messing with on this thing will bury you once they find out you're messing in their business."

Bolan ignored the man, keeping a fist around the Beretta in the pocket of his trench coat.

He'd left the Corvette in town after taking care to wipe it down, wanting to make sure none of the informants he'd had in the car earlier would be printed and picked up. Though they didn't know him for who he truly was, investigators following his trail would pick up on the fact that he was interested in the new cocaine connections that were flooding the city. Of course, they might draw those conclusions anyway, once they realized he'd snatched Cullen, but they wouldn't be so quick to think he was tracking the source of the pipeline down.

There were other agencies interested in the cocaine flow. The DEA people, operating under FBI sponsorship, were on the scene, trying to coordinate activities through the local branches of law enforcement. Bolan had seen some of their agents earlier in the day, still keeping watch on different routes that had been used for shipments during the past few weeks, hoping to catch the smugglers in a repeated maneuver. Desperate people were involved in the operation—desperate individuals trying to turn a profit on the trafficking and desperate cops trying to put those individuals out of business.

Law enforcement agencies hadn't been moving well on this one. So far almost a dozen men, including three members of the Coast Guard, had been killed by the smugglers. Two undercover cops had been found murdered in public places with Colombian neckties. Two more were still to be found.

Bolan didn't figure they would be.

He looked over his shoulder to see if anyone seemed to be taking undue interest in them. It was just past midnight, and a pale silver moon hung only a little above the blue-black of the ocean. People were still moving around the main marina area almost two hundred yards away. Lights swayed in the distance, hanging from the decks of the yachts and houseboats tucked into the pier so closely together. Strains of music filtered into the unseasonably chill night air, echoing the loneliness that lay over the oceanfront.

"So, what're you gonna do, tough guy?" Cullen asked, twisting to peer at Bolan. "Find a good place to shoot me and get the job done?"

Bolan gave him a cold glance, already sick of the man. Cullen's record ran the gamut of reprehensible sins and only showed an increased aptitude for upper management in recent years. Getting ready to make the move from enforcement and management for the Outlaws to a more legitimate facet of the gang's businesses.

"If I'd wanted you dead," Bolan answered, "you'd be dead by now." Cullen stumbled in the loose sand and went down. Bolan stopped, hanging back and keeping the Beretta trained on the man. Cullen cursed but made no move to gain his feet.

"Get up," Bolan ordered. "And don't repeat this."

"It would be a lot easier if I wasn't wearing these brace-lets," Cullen grumbled.

"You get to wear those for the dumb stunt you pulled back at the bar," Bolan said. "If they keep you from get-ting too brave, maybe I won't have to shoot you."

Cullen pushed himself to his knees and stood up. "How much farther?"

"Not much."

"You said that ten minutes ago."

"You know," Bolan said, "you might consider the fact that your nuisance value is going to exceed your worth to me if you don't give your mouth a rest."

Cullen gave him a lopsided grin and started walking again. "Just a reflex action, you know. Kind of keeps my mind off that little itch at the base of my skull that keeps waiting for the bullet."

"Like I said, Cullen, play your cards right, and there's not going to be a bullet."

Cullen snorted in derision. "Yeah, like spilling my guts to you is gonna keep me alive."

"It's something to consider."

"Sure."

"It kept you alive back at the bar." The wind swept in off the water, carrying a briny scent and plastering the trench coat around Bolan's legs. He fell into place behind his pris-oner.

"Where are we headed?"

"The boat house just ahead."

"Why didn't you just drive there instead of leaving the car two miles away?" Cullen asked, referring to the backup rental Bolan had sequestered under another name. "Or do you just like slogging through this shit in the middle of the night?"

Bolan didn't answer. He played the scene at the tavern over again in his mind. No matter how he looked at it, it hadn't made sense that so many police cruisers just happened to be in the area. An undercover tag team monitoring Cullen's activities was something he could accept. But the uniformed police had been ready for a heavy engagement. There was no reason for it, unless they had gotten wind that an unidentified force was rolling on this one with them. That would provide an explanation. And maybe he had been given up by one of the informants he'd contacted. He was directly engaging the operation himself at an earlier stage than he would have liked, but the pace wasn't going to slow down to let him find his stride. It was going to be a devilish tightrope walk until he could find a handle on the operation concerning the cops and the cocaine cowboys. At the moment, he had his hands on more information concerning trafficking in the area than Aaron Kurtzman showed on his computers.

"What kind of deal can we work out here?" Cullen asked.

"I'm not offering a negotiable deal," Bolan replied. "You'll take what I give you."

"And what is that?"

"You get to live."

"Sweet Jesus, but you're a generous son of a bitch."

"Care to try for the other option and see how you like that?"

"Is this some kind of takedown?" Cullen asked. "'Cause if it is, I can steer you away from this gig, man, 'cause this is a heavy number."

"I already know that, Skip. I just need the names of some of the players."

"Maybe you figure I know more than I really do. What happens then?"

"Come on, Skip, everybody knows you're top dog for the Outlaws. You going to try to make me believe you don't know who you're doing business with?"

Cullen stopped and turned around.

Bolan mirrored the movement.

"If I tell you what I know, I'm a dead man."

Bolan's voice was low and unforgiving. "You're that already, guy. I'm here to assure you of a new lease on life. If you come across with the names I need."

Mopping nervously at his bloody face with his manacled hands, Cullen said, "I got a cigarette inside my jacket. You mind if I smoke?"

"Go ahead." Bolan had patted the biker down before switching cars.

Cullen fumbled a cigarette pack from his shirt pocket and lit up. He breathed out smoke in twin plumes that were swept away by the ocean breeze. "You don't give a guy much choice—you know that?"

Bolan gave him a grim smile. "You know the score, Skip. Never offer anybody a deal unless it's a deal you want them to take."

"Yeah." Cullen sucked on the cigarette again. "Yeah."

"This deal's got an expiration date on it, too."

Cullen nodded as if he understood. "You know about the delivery tonight, too, huh?"

Bolan didn't, but he said he did anyway.

"You must have yourself some ears, pal."

"The clock's ticking, Skip."

Pained indecision etched across Cullen's face, made hollow and fleshless by the pale moonlight. "If I tell you what I know, and I mean everything, what am I buying myself?"

"The chance to feel the wind on your face in the morning when the sun comes up. For a lot of people, that's enough."

"It's enough for me, too, so you don't have to worry that I'll sell you out as soon as I get the chance."

"What do you have to sell, Skip? You don't even know who I am."

The cigarette made a bright orange coal in Cullen's cupped hands. "If you were a cop, I wouldn't even talk to you now. If you weren't as good at handling yourself as you are, I wouldn't talk to you. And if the guy I'm about to give you hadn't sold my ass down the river a few years back, I wouldn't talk to you, either." He smiled, but it was a clumsy artifice of real pleasure. "So, in a manner of speaking, you're gonna be helping me see to it the asshole gets what he deserves."

Bolan listened, sifting through the mixture of flattery and rationalization for details, fleshing out what he'd already learned as he mentally adjusted his sights on the next hell-zone.

WORKING THE SAILS and tiller easily, Bolan let the gentle wind push him toward the target area. The sloop was almost twenty-five feet long and sleek, cutting through the dark water in near silence.

The quietness of the night and the sea was refreshing, and Bolan couldn't help noticing it. There was a certain sense of aloneness that always seemed to come with the territory when he'd set foot on a sailboat; a sweet-and-sour ache that impressed itself on him, reminding him that the craft was an island tossed out on a hungry sea and survival depended on skill. The feeling seemed to be lost when it came to the bigger ships, but perhaps it was only the presence of the other people involved.

Or maybe it only seemed obvious to him because his life's path could be likened to that of the sailboat. Mack Bolan had never run with the safety of numbers. And those numbers were even fewer now, though the stakes sometimes appeared to be higher than ever. His life, as he had charted it, was spread across a sea of political and criminal strife that was every bit as dark and ominous as the one he sat on top of now.

The sea had its monsters, and the one he had tracked to its lair now was belching up white-powdered death on the Miami shore.

He trimmed the sails and felt the forward progress of the sloop come to a gliding halt as he reached for his binoculars. Fitting them to his eyes, he searched the near shore for the yacht Cullen had named.

Cool winds curled around him, and he knew they would have made him shiver if it hadn't been for the insulated blacksuit he wore.

There had been a few other craft moving across the black ocean surface, but he'd been careful to tack away from them without rousing interest.

Uneasiness squirmed through his mind and, despite his attempts, he couldn't brush it away. He tried to put a finger on what was bothering him and came up with a blank. Still, he trusted those senses he'd honed in the jungle, knowing they were as much a part of whatever arsenal he carried into battle as any piece of equipment he'd ever used.

Cullen's story had rung true. The biker hadn't been privy to everything about the cocaine operation or its extent, but he had known names. One of them belonged to the yacht Bolan searched for now, and another was the owner's.

The problem was, Bolan felt sure the yacht owner knew a name closer to the top.

The pipeline had been carefully organized, leaving only a slender thread that stretched in either direction of whatever routes the deliveries took. And enough middlemen were employed to make discovery of the entire operation almost impossible. In Colombia the sources were protected by machete and automatic weapons, buried deep in the jungle. In Miami the brokers were protected by subterfuge and bribery, buried deep in bureaucratic red tape.

Every time the federal and local police made a move to uncover the Miami connection, the buyers and brokers knew about their plans in advance and were able to avoid discovery. And brave law enforcement people were losing their lives as well as the war as the losses they suffered escalated.

Bolan saw it as a logistics problem of supply and demand. Whoever was ultimately at the Miami end of the operation was making enough money not to be greedy about it and to spread it around as a safety cushion.

Only the Executioner didn't have to sidestep the red tape or worry about the political clout that might be directed at him. His concerns revolved around the police agencies he was aiding. Without their knowledge.

He smiled grimly as he refocused the binoculars on the target vessel.

Even if Brognola had been able to erect some sort of cover that would allow him access to the current investigations on tap in Miami, that cover would have been bound to a certain extent by the same strictures that applied to the law enforcement people already involved. By calling his own shots on his attack on the enemy, he knew he was running more risks. But the chances for immediate success went up, as well.

The yacht was the *Swift Tiger* and was almost seventy feet of expensive combing and flash. According to Cullen, the yacht originally hailed from the Georgia coastline before the owner found a berth in the cocaine action in Florida and the Keys. She was owned by Harlan Duncan, though Cullen assured Bolan that was not the name on the paperwork involved in the yacht's title.

Duncan was a wild man who'd spent time in South Africa as a mercenary until he's saved up enough cash to purchase the yacht and buy his way into his first drug enterprise. Since then, according to Cullen, the man had learned to be careful and became more choosy about operations he became involved with. He had a rep as a shooter when things came down to the wire, and for knowing who to sell out. The only mistake made by Duncan was when the man unloaded Cullen on the Dade vice cops during a buy-back from a racket supplied by the confiscated drugs of two police departments in the area. The police departments had since cleaned house, and Duncan had gone on to brighter horizons before being implicated in the operation.

Bolan intended to dim those horizons tonight.

The *Swift Tiger* had settled into a public berth for now, setting up for what Cullen had designated as a major buy for a group of out-of-town bikers called Death's Enforcers.

The earlier uneasiness drifted over Bolan again as he surveyed his target. Duncan was a known trafficker, yet no one had seemed able to lay a glove on him.

He turned it over in his mind, searching for the reason for the uneasiness. No one could touch Duncan, although Cullen obviously knew more about the man's operation than what seemed reasonable if the trafficker was doing a quiet business. Some of the informants Bolan had talked with earlier in the day had also mentioned Duncan's name, though they hadn't known about the buy tonight.

The guy's operation wasn't exactly a secret, Bolan reflected as he examined the vessels closest to the *Swift Tiger* and failed to find anything that would trigger his combat sense. Cullen had even known about the buy set up by the Death's Enforcers bikers.

Then Bolan realized he'd found the source of his uneasiness. How could the law enforcement people involved in the investigation not know about Duncan and the prearranged buy if so much Intel was on the streets of the city?

He didn't know the answer to that; all he knew was that it didn't scan.

No matter how he tried to turn it around in his mind, it didn't seem possible that the agencies scooping out the new cocaine pipeline could have overlooked Duncan. Not unless people in those agencies were accepting payoffs and had kicked dirt over Duncan's name every time it turned up.

That was possible but not probable. You couldn't keep that kind of suppression up for long without being found out. And it seemed even less likely when he took into consideration the fact that the Miami PD had reacted so quickly to shut down the activity at the Red Rooster. Clearly they'd been geared to shut down any biker-related problems tonight.

Light rain started to fall, and he grimaced, knowing that if it got any worse it would definitely be a drawback in any action he took against the *Swift Tiger*.

So, if the law enforcement people knew about Duncan and perhaps the buy tonight, the *Swift Tiger* was the bait in a sucker play.

But who was the intended victim?

It could play any of a number of ways, Bolan told himself as he put the binoculars away and started filling out the sail. If the DEA or Miami PD was behind the suck, it meant someone had gotten to Duncan. That could mean they'd given up, at least for the moment, any hope of nailing the upper crust of the pipeline in order to make a big strike against the bulk of the operation. In which case, it wouldn't matter who the victim was as long as there was someone who could be made an example of. Maybe the Death's Enforcers bikers were just going to be in the wrong place at the wrong time.

And it could be a reverse suck.

The thought left Bolan colder than the wind and the rain.

As a reverse suck, it could be used to expose—if not kill outright—many of the law enforcement people involved in the investigation.

Either way, the impending action on the shoreline figured to be a bloodbath once someone kicked open the door.

Catching the wind, he guided his sailboat closer to the shore and the *Swift Tiger*, squinting through the heavier rain. Lightning flashed through the dark clouds skimming into view, followed a slow eight-count and later by a long peal of thunder.

Taking a berth along the dark wall of the pier, he dropped anchor and tested the boat motor. It caught easily. Satisfied, he covered it and went below.

The cabin was cramped, and there wasn't enough room to stand up straight. He filled the pockets of the blacksuit with extra magazines for the Desert Eagle and Beretta, garrotes, a folding knife and other necessary items. After pulling the black trench coat back on, he dropped three grenades in the voluminous pockets and added a navy blue yachting cap to make people remember him as wearing a dark cap rather than having dark hair. He slung an Uzi under his left arm, then pulled the trench coat over it. Then he headed back up to the deck and the rainstorm that was rolling in.

If there was a war in the makings, he intended to be ready for it and to make his presence count for something. And to salvage whatever he could from it that might move him up the next rung of the pipeline.

THE RAIN CONTINUED to fall, turning from a heavy sprinkling of needlelike drops to driving sheets that galed across the marina. Jagged streaks of lightning carved sizzling, white-hot arcs across a sky that had turned darker than the roiling water below it.

Bolan shifted, hunkering down to take advantage of the trench coat's length and to remain in the shadows piled atop the boat repair shop he'd chosen for his observation post. Thunder crackled on the heels of more lightning. At least the rain was warm.

Taking his binoculars from a pocket of the trench coat, he scanned the deck of the *Swift Tiger* again. No movement. Apparently Duncan and his crew had decided to batten down the hatches and wait the storm out. Or at least not put in an appearance until the Death's Enforcers came calling.

He wondered how Duncan would have felt if he suspected another storm was brewing on the heels of the one that was rocking his yacht at present.

It had taken Bolan forty-five minutes to make a recon of the area without drawing attention to himself. He hadn't found all the people involved, but he'd placed enough of them to know Duncan's craft was going to be the prize in a grim contest that night.

At least fifteen law enforcement people were ensconced in the darkness below, with two snipers backing their play from rooftops of different heights.

Thunder pealed and took away sound for a moment.

Bolan moved through the recon again, remembering the details about the area that he'd implanted in his mind. He could reach out mentally and touch each one. The worn wooden planking, fronting the marina area proper, that scuffed under his boot soles; the neon lights of the various taverns and restaurants in the area, which catered to the tourists, that would be visible even if fog rolled in from the sea; the casual conversations of the frequent passersby; the smell of ozone and brine in the air. It was all there in his mind, cataloged and carefully filed away for future reference.

Angling the brim of the yacht cap down a little farther as protection against the driving rain, he turned the binoculars toward the woman he'd spotted earlier.

He hadn't placed her in the scheme of things yet, and she remained a mystery. But there was no mistaking the interest she had in the *Swift Tiger*. As a guess, he had figured her to be part of the DEA team.

Lightning flashed without warning, washing away all color and reducing the marina to a black-and-white world for the next few seconds.

The woman was tall, Bolan judged from her surroundings, perhaps as much as six feet and surely no less than five-ten. Her attitude set her apart from her companions as much as her gender. She seemed apprehensive about the stakeout, whereas the others Bolan had spotted appeared to be only restless.

Bolan took her features in as she turned to gaze back along the winding street that led to the marina. Fine bone structure, wide-set eyes, short-cropped auburn hair. She wore a raincoat but didn't have it buttoned, revealing a dull gray sweatshirt, jeans and dark tennis shoes.

He was puzzled as he watched her speak briefly into a walkie-talkie. If the unit was sure the cocaine was aboard the *Swift Tiger*—as they evidently were—they should have been closing in for the bust. What made the Death's Enforcers so important that they had to be brought down along with Duncan? It was unclear to Bolan what the law enforcement team planned to do if the motorcycle gang showed up in force—unless they had information guaranteeing that the bikers wouldn't. That line of thinking brought even more questions to mind about what direction had the Intel been funneled from concerning the buy. Cullen had told him the Death's Enforcers were from Toronto, which was a long way from home for them. It was quite a distance to transport cocaine, especially if there were as many leaks about the buy as there appeared to be. Cullen was in the know, as were most obviously the locals and the DEA.

Bolan had to surmise there was even more buried under the surface of the operation than what was immediately apparent.

Before he could explore the complexities of his new line of thinking, the flat, blatting noise of a half-dozen motorcycle engines blasted through the night.

Shifting the binoculars, he switched to a wide-angle view on the winding road leading to the marina.

The motorcycles rode two abreast, their headlights uncertain in the falling rain. The riders' leather jackets looked dark and heavy with accumulated moisture.

Glancing back at the positions the law enforcement people were holding, Bolan watched flickers of dark movement and could sense the tension building in the ranks below.

A handful of umbrellas floated across the service road separating the docking area of the marina from the businesses. One paused, tipped back long enough for Bolan to see the teenage girl's face beneath it, then hurried on once she realized her route would intersect the bikers' path if she dawdled.

Training the binoculars back on the yacht, Bolan saw a shadow appear on the *Swift Tiger*'s deck, then fade.

The motorcycles came to a halt on the concrete parking area above the yacht's slip. The lights and engines switched off as the riders stumbled from their bikes. Their gestures suggested a swirl of curses on the air as most of the riders waved their arms and shook their heads in visible anger.

One of the bikers separated from the group, and Bolan brought him into sharp relief with the Bausch & Lombs. The man was tall and lean, with a long stride that seemed confident. He paused halfway down the metal steps leading to the docking area and gave orders. Bolan could tell that from the way the remainder of the group reacted. Three of the five Death's Enforcers members spread out in an obvious maneuver designed to guard the area.

To his left Bolan saw the nearest police sniper elevate his weapon slightly, evidently making a target selection. The man tapped a walkie-talkie lying on the rooftop by the butt of the rifle.

Bolan checked the other positions he'd marked on his mental map. He found that nobody moved to secure the area.

An uncomfortable itch started between his shoulder blades. If it looked like a duck, sounded like a duck and smelled like a duck, then obviously it was a duck. So what made the stakeout not a stakeout?

Someone switched on an electric lantern on the *Swift Tiger* and a weak yellow cone splashed against the deck.

Using the light available, wishing he had a Star-Tron scope to study the situation, Bolan memorized the face of the biker gang's leader. The guy looked to be in his early thirties, bearded and long-haired, but there was a quality about him that set him apart from the others.

The Death's Enforcers' leader vanished inside the yacht, followed by two of his men.

Bolan peered over the binoculars, taking in the full view of the scene.

Why weren't the law enforcement squads moving in? The parties they could nab in the drug buy were in the net, and the risk of innocent people getting caught in the cross fire was lower than it would have been if the storm hadn't blown in.

Sails ballooned from the masts of the other boats around the *Swift Tiger* as wire and rope riggings rattled in response.

Bolan watched the time pass on his watch, taking brief glances at the luminous hands under his sleeve. Lightning flashed and created mirror images in the puddles gathered across the rooftop in front of him.

It didn't make sense for the stakeout members to wait.

Unless some of the *Swift Tiger*'s crew had spotted the personnel involved as the soldier had. Duncan was an ex-merc. It didn't take a great leap of imagination to think the man was still as security conscious now as he had been in his South Africa days.

But if Duncan knew, would he still remain in the berth?

Bolan fitted the glasses back to his eyes and searched for the mystery woman, realizing Duncan would stay in the area if he'd dumped the cocaine in the sea and knew he had nothing to worry about when the bust went down.

The flaw in that deduction was that Cullen had said the amount of cocaine the Death's Enforcers members were buying was considerable. Would Duncan be willing to lose that much money?

Bolan didn't think so.

The woman looked more apprehensive than ever. She had crouched a little farther down behind the vehicle she'd taken cover behind. But every line of her body told Bolan she was apparently expecting the worst.

Putting the glasses away, Bolan returned to his surveillance of the yacht. Waiting, just like everyone else. He felt disgusted. If he'd been on his own in this one, he could have already penetrated Duncan's defenses and perhaps gotten his hands on the information he needed.

As it was, even if Duncan wasn't killed as a result of tonight's activities, the man would at least become the property of whatever law enforcement agency was heading up the stakeout.

Or whatever the hell the gathering was below.

The door of the yacht opened again, and the three bikers came back on deck carrying saddlebags, followed by a large bulky man in a Japanese-style robe. He clapped one of the bikers on the back and grinned, obviously enjoying the role of host.

Bolan tried to sort it out as he watched the three bikers walk up the metal steps. Okay, if Duncan didn't know about the police teams waiting in the darkness, why were those teams waiting to spring the trap?

Just as the bikers were converging on their motorcycles, a shot rang out and staggered one of them.

Bolan dragged the Uzi out, snapping off the safety as he brushed away the tails of the trench coat.

Hoarse shouts came in response.

The bikers scrambled, two of them lifting the wounded man onto a motorcycle behind the driver as the deep thunder of Harley engines coughed to life. More shots slammed through the night as the police unit sluggishly came to life.

The slow reaction speed of the surveillance teams told Bolan at once that someone had broken a holding order. The shot had sounded like one of the sniper rifles of the two men he'd spotted earlier, but he couldn't be sure which one with the wind and thunder masking the direction of the sound.

On board the yacht Duncan abandoned the deck in favor of the churning water. Bolan watched the ex-merc hit the surface of the ocean and cursed, launching into full stride as he tried to keep the man in sight. Duncan was the connection he needed to the next layer of the pipeline. Pumping his legs as hard as he could, he leaped from the roof he was on to the roof of a small café. The trench coat billowed out behind him, threatening to become tangled. He landed roughly, rolling across the rock-and-tar surface of the café. A shiver of autofire chased him, chipping pits in the tar: one of the police snipers had seen him.

Knowing the time for the high ground was at an end, he got his feet under him again and ran for the side of the building overlooking an alley that spilled out onto the marina street. Sparks flared from some of the roof rocks as another round whined off into the night.

Without breaking stride, he dropped over the edge onto the top of the Dumpster he'd seen in his earlier recon, then stepped quickly into the alley proper. Taking up a position at the corner of the building, he evaluated the action unfolding around the *Swift Tiger*.

A biker with a machine pistol gripped in both hands was raking the front of the building where the closest police sniper was. The other Death's Enforcers had scattered, choosing separate routes out of the immediate area.

Where would Duncan go? Bolan crossed the street at a dead run, knowing his dark clothing would prevent the snipers from knowing whose team he was on.

Lead hail from at least four weapons caught the biker and deposited him in a loose heap near the two motorcycles.

Hand-held searchlights probed the yacht's deck, brushing across the figures scattering toward the railing.

Bolan took cover in the vehicles near the area where he had seen the lady cop. Someone had a bullhorn and was bellowing orders in a harsh, angry voice, directing half his attention to the people on the *Swift Tiger* and half to the cops under his command. From controlled surveillance to fiasco in seconds. The disgust filled Bolan again as he crept through the parked cars.

Screams tore through the night, punctuated by the exchange of shots coming from the yacht and the surveillance team.

A flash of auburn hair caught his attention, diverting it for a moment from the choppy surface of the sea around the *Swift Tiger*.

Swiveling around the Ford Bronco next to him, Bolan watched the woman racing toward the fallen biker. Her tight features told him she had only one purpose on her mind and hadn't noticed the dark figure rising up from the ocean with a stainless-steel pistol clenched in its fist.

Bolan recognized Duncan immediately and moved out when he saw he couldn't fire without hitting the woman as she passed between them. He threw himself at her as Duncan locked into target acquisition, knowing death was only a heartbeat away.

3

Bolan reached for the woman and covered her with his body as his forward momentum spilled them to the hard concrete.

She fought against him, driving a sharp elbow into his ribs even as he struggled to free the Uzi. He caught the muzzle-flash of Duncan's weapon in the same second he felt the pain rip along his side.

The machine pistol came free as the ex-merc fired again, scarring the concrete by Bolan's head. Cradling the weapon in both hands, the Executioner squeezed the trigger. The Uzi snarled, and a line of 9 mm parabellums smashed into Duncan's chest, blowing the man backward.

Angry with the way the situation had turned out, Bolan rolled off the woman and recharged the machine pistol. The firing on board the yacht hadn't been dimmed by the shouted commands of the police.

"Are you okay?" he asked her.

"Fine," she said with a small nod. She appeared visibly shaken by the close call but seemed more interested in getting to the fallen biker.

Bolan followed her, wanting to get as close as possible to the main thrust of the action without standing apart from the crowd. If Bolan acted as though he belonged with the woman, most of the others shouldn't question his presence. At least for a little while, or until her real partners noticed him. It was a variation on the role-camouflage skills he'd perfected during his tours in Vietnam—becoming a part of the accepted background and fading into unimportance. But the marina was a hot spot, and no matter how good he was, he knew his time there was limited.

Squad cars rocketed down the marina street with sirens wailing, and the flashing light bars reflected splinters of color in the windows of the nearby businesses.

Pausing beside the dead biker, Bolan watched the police assault team close in on the yacht.

"Help me," the woman said as she tugged on the corpse. Her voice sounded hoarse, strained.

Bolan knelt and grabbed a fistful of leather jacket. He tugged and the body flipped over in response.

"Thank God," she breathed. Her relief was obvious as she tilted her head back. Tears mixed in with the raindrops.

"Did you think it was someone you knew?" Bolan asked.

She looked at him, control slipping into place behind the dark eyes. Her hand found her pistol where she'd laid it on the ground beside the corpse.

Bolan recognized it as the Smith & Wesson stainless-steel 10 mm the FBI had recently adopted for field operatives, telling him his guess about her probable DEA connections were dead on target. But who had she believed the dead biker to be?

The Smith & Wesson came up slightly in her hand, not enough to be a threat, but enough to remind him it was still there. "Who are you?" she demanded.

"Mike Belasko," Bolan said, knowing Brognola could drop the familiar alias into the cocaine investigation easily if it became necessary.

"I don't know you," she said. Her words were a challenge.

"I don't know you, either, lady." Bolan waved toward the yacht. "Hell, I don't know about most of this. I just walked in on this scene."

"And happened to be carrying an Uzi?"

Bolan shook his head as if in disbelief at her attitude. "Look, lady, I'm not expecting any pat on the head for saving your ass back there, but I'd at least expect you to be decent about it. Hell, I nearly got my own ass shot off trying to save yours."

"Can it, Belasko. Who the hell do you work for?"

"The Coast Guard."

"And you just happened to be in the area?"

Bolan snorted with annoyance, playing his role as a macho cop to the hilt. "Look, sister, I'm on vacation. I got a boat back there and was thinking about a late-night snack to wait out the storm when I noticed you guys huddled around the *Swift Tiger* looking like you were ready to sack the quarterback. If I butted into a private party, I'm goddamn sorry about it. But what's done is done. I slipped back to my boat, picked up a little artillery and decided to see what was going down for myself. The *Tiger*'s not exactly unknown to us, you know."

The woman got to her feet. "Did you ever think about calling someone about this setup before you jumped in, Belasko?"

"I didn't have time, lady. Before I realized for sure what was going down, all hell broke loose and I saw that guy ready to blow you away. I get the chance next time, I'll be sure and give the good guys a call first. That suit you?"

For a moment Bolan thought she was going to lose her temper. Then she mumbled an obscenity and turned away from him, heading for the area where Duncan had gone back into the water.

Not wanting to lose the flimsy credibility her presence lent him, Bolan followed, hoping for a chance to look things over for himself.

The assault squad had moved in on the yacht now, kicking in the door and demanding all hands on deck. At least a dozen people, male and female, were lying facedown on the bullet-pocked surface.

"That was Duncan you shot, wasn't it?" the woman asked when she noticed him behind her.

"Yes, ma'am," Bolan said, glancing around at the crowd that started to gather by the police cruisers.

"Where?"

Bolan moved ahead and knelt on the wooden railing where he'd shot Duncan. A dark blob floated only inches below the surface of the water. He leaned forward, reaching for it, twisting his fingers in the wet silk, then guiding the floating weight gently upward and inward.

"Oh, my God!" a feminine voice shrilled.

Glancing up, Bolan saw a teenage girl in a bikini standing on the deck of a nearby houseboat and staring at the corpse he was pulling from the water.

"Sergeant!" The woman's voice at his side was harsh and imperative as she stood and yelled to the nearest cop in a yellow rain slicker.

The cop glared at her.

"Get this area cordoned off *now*, Sergeant. Tell those people this is not a public event they can stand around and gawk at. Until we get the marina secured, we have to assume some of Duncan's people got away."

The cop stomped to the edge of the concrete wall. "Look, I don't need you telling me how to run my job. I don't know who the hell you think you are, but—"

The woman cut him off. "Special Agent Piper Silverman, Sergeant, of the DEA. We're running this operation. If you'd listened at roll call instead of going for that last-minute nap maybe you'd be more on top of this situation. Now get the lead out."

Bolan paused, watching the cop to see how things were going to develop. For a moment it seemed undecided, then the cop moved off to issue orders to the other uniformed men. The mother of the girl on the houseboat came and took her away, and everything quietened down under the storm again.

Kneeling, Silverman extended a leg in the water, found something she could step on, then added her strength to Bolan's. The body seemed to come free immediately and landed on the wooden surface with a wet plop of loose-jointed limbs.

"Jesus," Silverman said as she looked at the ruin the 9 mm parabellums had made of the man's chest.

"It's worse on the other side," Bolan assured her. He studied her face in the uncertain splash of the lightning and spotlights being splayed over the marina. His estimate of her age had been about right. At close proximity he saw that she was probably a couple of years younger, and the anxiety that had been troubling her had left a dark shadow on her features.

"Are you always this cheerful, Belasko?" Silverman asked as she holstered her automatic in a shoulder rig.

"Some days are better than others," Bolan admitted.

"You're probably the kind of guy who likes to attend autopsies, too."

Bolan helped her pat the dead man down, wondering what had the woman so tense. "You two make a pretty good team, Silverman," he said.

"What two?"

"You and that chip on your shoulder."

"Get screwed, Belasko. This is a DEA case you god-damn local cowboys nearly fucked up. I don't need any goddamn comments about interdepartmental relations at the moment. You got a beef, take it up with your superiors."

"No beef. I'm on vacation, remember?"

"Yeah. And you should have kept your nose in your own business instead of trying to score a few brownie points here tonight."

"A couple of those points came in when I took this guy out for you."

She paused, leaning forward.

Bolan could sense the brittleness covering her emotions and was puzzled by her tension. Evidently she wasn't new in the field. She handled the uniformed police with too much experience for that.

"Yeah, well, at the time you were racking 'em up, Dead-eye, did you happen to think we might have wanted this asshole alive?"

He didn't speak, waiting to see how she was going to handle the situation she was forcing.

She broke eye contact and looked away, her lower lip trembling slightly with the effort of keeping the emotions in. When she looked back at him, her eyes were misty. "Hey, look," she said in a more sedate tone, "I was out of line there. It's not you or even this dead lump here. It's just that I got a few other things on my mind right now. You understand?"

Bolan nodded.

"Help me get him turned over. I didn't find anything in his front pockets."

He flipped the body over and heard her gasp of surprise when she saw the exit wounds. Her hands shook when she reached for the pants pockets.

Bolan caught them gently and pushed them away. "Let me," he said. "You're going to have to look good for the photographers and press boys and the brief after this is finished."

"I've seen dead bodies before, Belasko," she said in a voice that was less cocky than before.

"Yeah, I know. It's that kind of job." For a moment he thought she was going to be stubborn about it, then saw the spark of defiance die in her eyes. "You're pushing yourself too hard tonight, lady," he said gently.

"It's that kind of job," she repeated.

"Yeah, well, take a breather for a minute and let me handle this. You can watch my hands and make sure I don't try to crib anything." Bolan went through the corpse's pockets with practiced ease, not expecting to turn anything up and not feeling surprised or disappointed when he didn't. He glanced back at the woman. "Duncan's clean. Probably left everything back on the yacht. What kind of ID do you need to manage a dope buy?"

"You seem pretty informed for a guy on vacation, Belasko. You know about Duncan and about the *Swift Tiger*."

Bolan shrugged. "Goes with the territory."

"Yeah, I guess it does." But her eyes still glowed with subdued suspicion. "Kind of makes me wonder what else you know about."

The quietness spun around them, as fragile as glass and promising to be full of cutting edges if it was broken in the wrong way. He glanced away from her, checking the movement on the *Swift Tiger* before she could ask any questions he wasn't prepared to field.

The law enforcement teams had swept across the deck, and the yellow slickers of the Miami Police Department were starting to dominate the numbers. Bolan knew his impromptu cover wouldn't hold much longer, but he hated to quit the killzone empty-handed. He wanted to uncover why the cops willingly let the bikers escape unscathed, with no signs of pursuit. Then there was Piper Silverman…who had she feared for? And the lead to Duncan's next link in the cocaine pipeline was missing. He knew at least some clues would be found on the yacht, but the marina was getting too hot too fast to provide a safe harbor for him. Once the initial reaction of the bust waned and immediate retaliation to opposing forces died away, the officers involved would start checking the people around them more closely. And he'd already made himself known to Silverman and the police sniper who had tried to take him out. The situation was rapidly becoming more explosive.

"I hope you didn't have anywhere to go real soon, Belasko," Silverman said as she got to her feet, "because I want to ask you a few questions."

"I'm on vacation, lady."

"Yeah, well it seems to me you took yourself off vacation when you decided to draw cards against the hand being played out here tonight."

"Getting to spend the rest of the night with the Feds and the local cops isn't exactly my idea of walking away a winner."

Silverman glanced at Duncan's body deliberately. "At least you're walking away, Belasko."

"I suppose so."

"Anyway, clear everything up with the shooting teams and you'll probably be free to go."

"Thanks," Bolan said. But he didn't believe her. He could see the curiosity and doubt lingering in her eyes, and knew she wasn't going to let his presence on the scene slide that easily.

"Silverman!" The harsh male voice bellowing the woman's name carried a lot of authority as it cut through the shallow winds gliding through the marina.

Silverman looked up and Bolan followed her gaze.

A squat, powerfully built man separated himself from the crowd leaving the deck of the *Swift Tiger*. The upturned collar of the dark raincoat almost met the brim of his sharply creased fedora, leaving doubts about the existence of any neck at all. He came to a sudden halt at the end of the parking area overlooking the wooden walkway. He stared at Duncan's body and said, "Shit."

Bolan got to his feet, aware that the man was giving him more than a casual inspection.

"That Duncan?" the man asked as he cupped his hands and lit a cigar. The lighter gleamed silver briefly, held captive in the man's thick, blunt fingers, then blossomed into a floating yellow-gold stream that ignited the cigar tip into an orange coal.

Silverman nodded, brushing wet hair back from her face.

"Nice piece of work, Silverman," the man commented, his hoarse voice full of sarcasm. "Your idea?"

"Hell, no," the lady Fed responded as she gripped the edge of the railing facing the parking area and pulled herself up. "Meet Belasko, one of the Coast Guard's local heroes and representative of the Miami movement for law and order, complemented by a fast gun."

"What the hell is he doing here?" the man asked as Silverman swung up to face him.

"How the hell should I know, Judson? This is supposed to be your goddamn operation, remember? I'm just supposed to sit back and file my nails while the senior member of this team coordinates everything."

Bolan saw the shadows spread over Judson's face and twist it up like a fist.

"One of the local glory boys you cut into this operation almost cost us big tonight by opening fire before the bikers got clear," Silverman yelled. "I want you to remember that. And if you don't, by God, I will."

"Careful, Silverman," Judson warned in a low voice, "you're treading awfully close to insubordination here."

"I can tread closer, Judson. I can tread insubordination all the way up to the review board if I have to. You either pull your head out of your ass on this operation now, or I promise you that's exactly where I'll head."

Bolan watched the tension between the two people escalate, showing in the solid jawline Silverman presented and in Judson's measured smoking motions. A small group of policemen had drifted nearby to overhear the heated debate, trying in vain to appear uninterested.

"You're out of line here, Silverman," Judson said in a soft voice Bolan had trouble hearing. "I suggest you remind yourself you're a responsible field agent and not some lovesick girl."

For a moment Bolan thought the woman was going to strike Judson. But the moment passed, and she jammed her fists in her coat pockets forcefully.

"Get fucked, Judson," she said through clenched teeth, then turned and strode away toward the yacht.

Judson grinned without mirth. He flicked ash from his cigar as he watched her walk away, then shifted his attention back to Bolan. "Coast Guard, huh?"

"Yeah. I'm on vacation." He hurried on before the DEA man could say anything else. "Gal's rough as a cob, ain't she?"

"She likes to think so."

"She was giving me hell just before you got here."

"Had every right to. What the hell is the Coast Guard doing involved in this?"

"It isn't exactly the Coast Guard. It's just me. I wandered into this by accident."

Judson rubbed his jaw as if trying to swallow the lie. "Yeah, yeah. Belasko, right?"

Bolan nodded affirmatively.

"You shoot Duncan?"

"Didn't give me a choice. Ask Silverman. Pissed off as she is right now, I think she'll still vouch for me."

"You better hope so, champ, because if she don't, I'm going to own your ass. And if it's not regulation Coast

Guard equipment, I'm going to boot it just as high as I can. You understand me?''

"Yeah."

The DEA man blew out a lungful of smoke and choked on a sudden cough. When he regained his breath, he said, "You stay right here with the body, Belasko, and don't you shift your ass away from this scene till I say it's okay."

Judson clamped the cigar between his teeth again and sucked it into flaring life for effect, letting the warm orange glow drift across his craggy features. Then he turned and stalked off to trail in Silverman's wake through the crowd of law enforcement people.

Bolan glanced at the crowd held at bay by the yellow-slickered policemen, noticing that crews from the local media had begun arriving on the scene. One reporter was being pushed bodily from the cordoned area after slipping through the ranks of the police. His voice was keening and shrill, protesting about First Amendment rights. The policeman escorting the reporter was the same sergeant Silverman had addressed earlier, and he wasn't being gentle.

Shifting the Uzi out of sight under the folds of the trench coat, Bolan saw the interest of the onlookers gradually veer toward him and the corpse at his feet. Minicams aimed at him as camera flashes splashed against the dark water in the periphery of his vision. At this distance he knew the pictures would be vague concerning his features and his identity, but that could change in a handful of seconds if the media people ever broke the police lines even for just an instant.

He reached into his pocket for his wallet as a yellow-slickered policeman walked toward him with a hand gripping the upper arm of a handcuffed, bikini-clad woman from the *Swift Tiger*. He dropped it open as the policeman drew even with him. "Fields," he said. "I'm with the

DEA." He shut the wallet before the policeman could glimpse the dark emptiness it held.

"What do you want?" the policeman asked.

"I'd like to change prisoners," Bolan replied, indicating the corpse at his feet.

The cop smiled and shook his head. "No way, Jack. I got a live one—I don't need a dead one. This lady's my ticket to a nice, warm and dry squad car while you guys sort everything out in the rain. I'm not interested."

"This isn't what you'd call a request, guy," Bolan said in a firm voice as he stepped to prevent the policeman from moving on. "Judson is going to want to talk to all the people from the yacht and wants us to see to it they're kept separate instead of being crammed into squad cars like cattle."

"Fuckin' DEA assholes," the cop mumbled.

"What was that, officer?"

The cop looked up at Bolan and glared. "Not a goddamn thing, sir. I'll be happy to exchange prisoners, sir, happy to stand out here in this goddamn rain for hours on end guarding this scumbag's body."

Bolan grinned as he slid his arm through the woman's in place of the cop's. She looked up at him doubtfully, flinching at his touch. She was young and dark haired, with the kind of lean body that complimented the bikini rather than being complimented. "Spoken like a trooper," he said as he guided his charge away.

"Horseshit," the cop said. "Sir."

"Look at it this way—maybe you'll get lucky and get your face plastered across *People* magazine or *Newsweek*."

"And take a chance on getting my ass blown away while I'm off duty by some two-bit pusher who recognizes me and thinks I'm an undercover officer? No, thank you."

Bolan led the woman up the steps to the parking area, searching the crowd down by the yacht for Silverman or Judson.

"Hey!"

Bolan looked over his shoulder at the young cop standing over Duncan's body.

"I want them cuffs back when you're through with them, ace. The DEA ain't so damn hard up they can't spring for the cost of a pair of their own."

Bolan waved at him reassuringly and hustled the woman through the police ranks. He paused by an unmarked car and drew the attention of the uniformed policeman standing in front of it. "I'm supposed to take her to the hospital," he told the cop. "She's tripping on something and Judson wants to make sure she stays alive. Somebody iced Duncan, and Judson figures she might be able to give us a line on Duncan's connections." He guided her inside the car as he talked.

"She looks okay to me," the officer said, peering after her.

"I wasn't aware we had any doctors moonlighting at the local PD," Bolan said dryly. "Just give me a minute and I'll go tell Judson you think it's just a false alarm." He settled behind the wheel and shut the door, rolling the window down.

"Get in the damn car," the officer said. He glared balefully.

Bolan smiled and dragged the flashing red light from the top of the car. "I'm in. Now, you want to see about getting me out of here?"

The cop put his hands on the door. "I'll be glad when you DEA shitheels clear out of the area and let us get back to real police work. If I'd been running this show, we'd have busted those bikers, too. What kind of arrangement you guys got with them anyway?"

"Ask Judson."

"Judson ain't telling nobody shit."

"You want to see about getting me out of here before it gets any more crowded?"

The cop made a face and shook his head. "Sure. Why the hell not? We done everything else for you guys we could. I tell you one thing, though—this is the first time I ever been on a bust with the DEA, and it's been a hell of a letdown. Next time I'm asked to put in some overtime to help cover one of these things, I'm going to try to call in sick."

Bolan shook his head in sympathy and watched the cop move away from the unmarked car as he rolled up the window. The yellow-slickered arms waved in opposite directions, like a raincoat-clad Moses parting a human sea. The Executioner hit the ignition and tapped the accelerator, placing the big car's bulk behind the cop to emphasize the man's commands. People moved and a path was made. He edged forward, taking time to glance at the small group gathered by an ambulance, parked near the yacht, with its doors open. Evidently the *Swift Tiger* hadn't been taken without cost. The whirling cherry-red slashes fell across the faces of Silverman and Judson, illuminating the fact that their personal argument still raged.

"Who are you?" the woman asked. She sat with her back against the passenger door, her arms cuffed behind her. Her dark eyes kept darting nervously from the crowd surrounding them to Bolan.

"For right now," Bolan said as he steered the big car around a news van, "I figure I'm maybe the best friend you got."

"You ain't no cop, guy. I saw your wallet when you buzzed the cop you took me from. You might've fooled and browbeat the junior woodchuck into believing you, but I know I didn't see no tin inside your wallet."

Bolan paused, waiting as the policeman cleared pedestrians to one side, then tapped the accelerator impatiently to slide through the brief opening. He watched it close behind him immediately in the rearview mirror.

"Ain't you going to answer me?" the woman asked.

"No."

"How about if I roll down this window and scream my lungs out?"

Bolan gained the street and made his way back toward the warehouse where he'd left Cullen bound and gagged. The area was hot, roasting even, but it was still wide open for infiltration. And he was betting neither enemy camp in Miami would be looking for him to stay in the marina area. Especially not when both were looking to recoup the losses suffered during the night.

"They're your lungs," he said as he dropped the window a couple inches to let in some of the cool night air. The car was stuffy and hot. "But you might ask yourself if you really want to spend the rest of the night answering questions for the local detectives and the DEA." He glanced at her and saw the indecision twist her features. "I figure you're a smart girl."

She slumped against the door and watched the wipers swish across the windshield. "I hope you're right," she said, then turned back to face him. "You aren't with Hunsaker, are you?"

"No." Bolan turned the name over in his mind, trying to find a niche for it unsuccessfully.

"In case you didn't know, Hunsaker is Duncan's boss. *Was*, I guess I should say. Duncan's dead now. But I guess you knew that."

"Yeah."

"It's funny," she went on. "I knew you weren't a cop the minute I laid eyes on you, but I don't figure you for one of Hunsaker's boys, either."

"I'm not." Bolan looked at her, stared into the dark eyes and watched her wet her lips nervously. "Hunsaker was Duncan's boss?"

"Yeah. I thought you knew that."

"No."

"That's why I figured you were one of Hunsaker's boys at first. Hunsaker's too used to dealing with people in the straight world, too used to hiring people to watch the people he hires. He figured Duncan would have fucked him over if he got the chance. He was right. Only Duncan never got the chance."

"Who's Hunsaker?"

The woman looked at him in wide-eyed disbelief. "Who the hell are you, mister?"

"A guy looking for answers," Bolan responded. "And I need them fast because the cops are going to be moving on this even faster."

"Aren't you some kind of competition? Duncan had told some of us that the local Mafia families were getting pissed off about the deal Hunsaker had set up with the Colombians. Then when I saw you take this car from the cop as bold as brass, I thought maybe you were one of the hard guys from the families. Duncan'd had some shit with them over the last few weeks, but he wasn't worried about it."

"Maybe he should have been."

"Yeah. Maybe he should have."

Bolan turned off the highway and coasted down a twisting road leading back to the marina. He came to a stop in a dark section of the black-topped parking area and switched off the ignition. The sailboat was a little over a couple of klicks back the way he had come. It wouldn't take long to get back there, and maybe most of the law enforcement teams would be gone by then. He knew he'd need some of the hard-punch ordnance he had stored aboard the boat once he got his sights refocused. The battle for Miami's newest high-profit shipping line was only heating up. When he looked back at the woman, he saw bright tears filling the dark eyes.

"So, what's it going to be? You going to leave me handcuffed and drop me in the ocean somewhere?" Her voice cracked as she spoke.

Bolan reached inside his trench coat.

The woman's eyes widened in fear as she glimpsed the hardware strapped across his body.

Taking a lock pick from the kit in an inside pocket, Bolan said, "Let me see those cuffs."

The woman moved as if she was made of disjointed sticks held together by baling wire. She trembled under his touch as he picked the lock, then she rubbed her wrists once he'd removed the handcuffs and tossed them into the rear seat.

Putting the lock pick away, Bolan retrieved five hundred dollars in big bills and spread them out on the seat between them. He smiled. "The deal is this—you tell me what you know about Duncan and the cocaine operation, and you get the five hundred and you walk. If I get the feeling you're lying to me, I'll handcuff you to this car and give the local cop shop a call and tell them where to find you."

"Hey, man, you won't get nothing but the straight shit from me. You can bank on it."

Bolan indicated the five hundred-dollar bills. "I already am."

4

Piper Silverman studied the fat lazy bubbles trapped inside the five-gallon bottle sitting on the water dispenser in the hallway of the police station. As she filled her plastic cup, she watched them form, slowly oozing free from the neck of the water bottle to wobble unsteadily upward. Rolling, sleekly fat, they floated out of control to smash against the top of the almost-full bottle. At the moment it seemed to her that her career was just like one of those bubbles, kicking free of the earthly shackles that made up most of her workdays to smash helplessly against the vicious upper crust of the Drug Enforcement Agency. Against Frank Judson.

She drank the water, so hyped-up on the events of the past few hours that her senses seemed to hover close to the point of overload. The coldness flooded her mouth in unaccustomed intensity, bringing a brief, biting pain to her throat as she swallowed. The smell of the plastic cup was rank, cloying, and gave the water an unpleasant aftertaste.

But the aftertaste was nowhere near as sharp or unpleasant as the one she got every time she thought of Judson.

She crumpled the cup and dropped it into the small basket beside the watercooler.

"Bad day?" a man's voice inquired.

She turned to face the speaker, logging his name with difficulty because everything else was on her mind so much. Roger Baskins was the local DEA agent and would have been running the Miami operation if Judson hadn't insinuated himself into it as coordinator for the group. She gave the man a wan smile. "More like a bad life," she responded with more feeling than she'd intended. Her hands still quivered when she thought how close the violence had come to reaching out for the innocents at the *Swift Tiger*. Too often her mind continued to play tricks on her, transposing the features of the dead biker with the ones of the man she'd feared had been lying there. She could still taste the bile at the back of her throat from having thrown up after achieving a brief respite from Judson's attention.

Baskins slipped a plastic cup from the supply mounted on the wall and filled it. "You got a real asshole for a supervisor, you know that?"

"Yes. I think half of the Florida law enforcement agencies know that by now."

Baskins's green eyes twinkled. "I really doubt the numbers are that high. Truth to tell, Judson's keeping a pretty tight lid on what went down at the marina."

"Too bad he couldn't control things there a little better, though."

"Are you talking about Duncan getting wasted?"

The ·image of the dead biker flickered through Silverman's mind again, causing goosebumps to race up her arms. She hugged herself, willing her mind away from the possibilities that had existed there and trying in vain to make herself believe those possibilities weren't increasing every moment. She nodded in response to the man's question. "None of it was worked out very well ahead of time, Roger. You were there. You saw how everything seemed to go down the tubes at once. Duncan's death is going to curtail the activity Judson promised the local heroes, and it's easy to see they're not going to take that lightly. The Miami PD has put a lot of man-hours into developing the *Swift Tiger* connection themselves."

"I know. Have you met Carruthers?"

"The guy heading up the local vice section?"

Baskins nodded. "The very one. He's not a nice man to screw around with, kid, and I don't think your supervisor has realized how thoroughly he's worn out his welcome in these parts."

"Carruthers isn't a happy camper, right?"

"Carruthers isn't anything but livid right now, Piper." Baskins refilled his plastic cup and glanced down the hallway.

Silverman followed his glance, listening to the clack of heels passing across the tiled floor of the hallway. Men and women in plainclothes and uniforms drifted in and out of different doorways. Most of them looked tired, and she knew the majority of them had been involved in the containment of the *Swift Tiger*, whether by being there in person or by covering extra shifts so others could be. Part of her, the part she tried to keep hidden when she worked in districts other than her own, felt sorry for them. The yacht's capture hadn't yielded much in the way of contraband— hardly enough to warrant mention in the media. Except that three officers fell in the brief exchange of gunfire. One of them wouldn't be getting back up.

She looked back at Baskins and saw hesitation move across the worn face of the older man. She picked up the uneasiness from the agent instantly, feeling it pierce her like icicles. "This isn't a chance meeting at the office watercooler, is it, Roger?"

He looked at her briefly, then looked away, speaking over her head but only at a volume loud enough for her to hear. "I got a friend in vice, Piper, who tells me Carruthers has organized a war party for the bikers who got away tonight. My friend tells me Carruthers is figuring on regaining some media points tonight by rounding them up."

"That son of a bitch!" Silverman noticed at least two people stare at her, then turn their attention back to their tasks. "Have you told Judson?"

Baskins made a sour face. "The way I figure it, nobody around here much owes Judson the time of day. He came down here waving Justice paper that gave him the right to a case the local people have been trying to build for some time and had the authority to let an out-of-state biker gang ride with an unspecified amount of cocaine that reduced the size of this bust to almost nothing. On top of that, people around here don't like Yankees, Piper."

"Are you counting yourself as one of the local people, Roger?"

He smiled, but she knew he was aware she saw through his pretense and it vanished from his craggy face. He drank more water. "You got to remember that I'm about as local as the DEA gets in this area."

"So we're dealing with a bunch of fragile egos here? Is that what you're trying to tell me?"

"Damn it, Piper, I like you. You're a hell of a smart lady. If I didn't think that and respect it, I wouldn't even be talking to you now. You don't need me to tell you that over half the drug justice done in the United States is more of a grab for political ratings points than anything else. You know how the system works—you make the collars and you get the funding. If you don't, your department starves. Even Bennett hasn't been able to change that since he's taken over the drug scene. Everybody wants a piece of the action. The Coast Guard, U.S. Customs, the DEA, the State Department, the Department of Defense, local police and sheriff's departments—all of these people are hustling the business with as much gusto as the street dealers are hustling the merchandise. Figure on the amount of labor the druggies put into doing X amount of dollars a year in sales, and you can balance it with the man-hours these different agencies invest in trying to cut just as deeply into those dollars as they can. It's a goddamn big business, Piper. Bureaucracy at its finest. If we could put a halt to the drug business today, how many people would you be putting out of jobs? Jobs that are more or less financed by the amount of cash and property those agencies seize every year from the people they hunt. Face it—the system we've established in the courts is to legally strip the pushers and dealers of anything and everything we can—like shearing sheep—then turn them loose so they can put it all back on again." He wadded his cup and threw it into the basket, refusing to meet her gaze.

"So, why tell me Carruthers is organizing something like this?"

"I've been around the block, Piper, and this old nose still works pretty good. I don't smell this as just a play by Judson for the glory involved, though you can bet your ass I wouldn't put it above him. The way I got it smelled out, I see you guys coming into the area because you got a man in deep somewhere in the pipeline. With all the territory Judson's stepped across on this thing, and the type of lawman you got down here in Miami fighting for the funding involved, I see you guys holding a lid on a pressure cooker that's going to explode in your face." Baskins paused to light a cigarette, then blew the blue-gray smoke at the stained ceiling overhead. "You're good people, Piper, and one of the best damn operatives I've seen in the agency, bar none. I care about you. You've done me a good turn down here now and then, and an old codger like me remembers that. I also care about that guy you people have put in deep down here in this mess. I've been deep a few times—it's no fun."

Silverman didn't say anything as she returned his gaze full measure. It was something she had learned early in her career and it had been a major stride toward equality in a business that was still predominantly male.

"You've been deep, haven't you, Piper?"

"A few times," she said, trying to keep her mind from reaching out for the scum-slick memories that squirmed uneasily with even that small admission.

"You know how it feels, then. Cut off, existing in a world you thought you'd somehow sidestepped, one that you had made a decision to never enter. Yet, amazingly, someone in the agency decides you're the best person to go deep and there you are. Trying to fit. Scares you how quick you can let all those layers of morality slip away from you, doesn't it?"

"I never let it slip that far, Roger," she said. But she was lying and hoped it didn't show. The shadowy world of the deep side was different, and it was all too easy to remember the effortless slide you could make to join the level of people you were hunting. Raw passions existed at that level. Extreme passions that seemed like an emotional free-fall once you were not bound by the restrictions imposed by society and whatever agency you'd aligned yourself with. Freedom. That was what it was. To survive deep you had to learn to shelve those learned responses of morality and operate on baser instincts. Loyalty became something to kill or die for instead of being a product bandied about by the bureaucratic standards of the agency. If you were good, and you had to be good to even attempt to survive deep, chances were you could carve a niche for yourself in that put-on life if you wanted to. Maybe better yourself economically, assume a better life-style, play a more dangerous game than you'd first signed on for because playing those games—living life on that sharp and bitter edge—could become the most fascinating facet of your life. And love. More often than not, you could find love in the eyes of someone you'd never had the chance to meet before and would never meet again. She still felt the bittersweet ache of some of those memories and knew she always would.

"Piper?"

She glanced back up at Baskins, noting the concerned look on the man's face.

"Are you okay?"

"Sure."

"You looked like you were somewhere else there for a minute."

Silverman hugged herself more tightly, willing away those memories of confusion, trying to avoid the intricate confusion of the situation facing her. Wishing she could deny her responsibility for everything that was happening now. "Maybe I was. But I'm back now. You're not going to tell Judson about Carruthers's war party?"

"I'd rather not be the one to let the cat out of the bag. After you and Judson fly back to New York, I'm still going to have to live with this guy." Baskins flicked ash off the end of his cigarette onto the floor and then stepped on it, reducing it to a gray powder. "Fact is, I was sort of hoping you could handle this by yourself without involving Judson. You know, kind of cue your deep guy on the sly without anyone knowing."

"I wish I could, Roger," Silverman said, and meant it.

Curiosity flared to green life in Baskins's eyes. "What are you talking about, Piper? I've turned some dirt on this operation you guys are heading up. Granted, there's not a hell of a lot of it, but I did find out you're the lifeline on this deep."

Silverman let her displeasure show, hoping it would keep Baskins at bay. She liked the man and didn't want to have to step on his toes. Especially not when the operation was still in Florida, and in view of the fact that Baskins might be dissuaded from making any further information contributions concerning local law enforcement efforts against Death's Enforcers. "You shouldn't have been able to get that much," she said.

Baskins shook his head, blew out an angry lungful of smoke as he looked away. He dropped his cigarette and crushed it out underfoot, jamming his hands deep in his pockets. "For Christ's sake, Piper, I'm not the enemy. We're on the same team."

"I know."

"You know?"

Silverman didn't say anything, feeling guilty that the man had been able to confide in her so much and she couldn't return the favor. Didn't want to, she amended. Damn it! At least be honest with yourself.

"You know?" Baskins's anger was evident in the way he held himself. "You know? Is that all you can say, Piper?"

"It is for now, Roger."

"Shit! Now I'm beginning to know how Carruthers feels. I didn't sign on to this operation just to get a polite thank-you and a hand job as I'm being shown out the door, kid. You got a serious problem brewing here because there's so many people anteing up for this pot. This isn't the time to be playing secrets. You hear what I'm saying?"

Silverman made her voice final and polite, ignoring the stab of guilt lancing through her bowels, trying to decide if the guilt had been a product of what she was doing to Baskins or what she had done to help weave the spider web of sudden death and betrayal into an even more confused pattern. "I'll try to keep your name out of it as much as possible, Roger, but I'll have to let Judson know what's going on locally."

Baskins stared at her in stony silence.

Silverman wanted to turn away but found herself unable.

"You can handle it without involving Judson," he said in a low voice. "You're the contact officer on this operation. Call your guy and tell him what the score is. Pull the plug on it if you have to. No deep is so important that we got to risk this much flak in interdepartmental relations. You get something like that rolling through the ranks, and you may not end up with enough left of your guy to make a decent ink blotter out of. You know I'm telling you the way it is.''

''You're right,'' she replied, letting some of the warmth drip back into her voice, hoping she could steer his thinking away from the darker perimeters of the operation. ''But it's not easy to get in contact with our guy right now. He's having to move in unfamiliar territory, and he's already seen evidence that the local police aren't exactly the most trustworthy allies he's worked with.''

Baskins was silent, staring into her eyes.

She tried to blank her mind of the guilt, wishing that sometimes you could go back and do things differently. But at the time, it had seemed so necessary, so vital, a reminder of life. So right. And yet so damnably wrong. She kept the tears from her eyes with effort.

''There's more to it than that, isn't there?'' Baskins said. ''No.''

''Bullshit, Piper. The first thing your deep would have done after seeing one of his compatriots go down under what was supposed to be friendly fire would be to call you guys at the first opportunity and ask what the hell was going down.''

''I've got to go see Judson,'' she said as she turned away, hoping she could disrupt the man's chain of thought.

Baskins closed a beefy hand around her upper arm, stopping her. She whirled around, feeling herself slide to the edge of control. Anger outweighed the confusion, threatening to goad her into a more physical response. ''Take your hand off my arm.''

The hand dropped away. ''What is it, Piper? What aren't you telling me?''

She tried to stare him down, failing because she knew she wasn't being backed by the inner sense of loyalty she demanded from people she worked with. To thine own self be true. She tried to live that when nothing else worked. When the marriage went bust. When the promotions didn't come through for her as easily as she felt they should have. When she looked out the windows of her apartment and wished there was someone else whose life would touch hers in ways she'd never experienced. The flush of guilt roiled over her in an almost physical presence. Images crowded into her mind, as did sensations of hands touching in the darkness, lips meeting, drinking in another ragged breath while searching for a solace she'd never known. She chased the mind pictures away, feeling her control fragment and slip. She maintained it, banished the guilt to deal with later.

"You can't get hold of the deep, can you, Piper?" Baskins looked incredulous.

She shook her head, not trusting her voice. Swallowed hard to loosen the muscles in her throat.

"That's it, isn't it?" Baskins was relentless.

Silverman recognized the investigator in the man now, a frantic beast trapped behind human eyes, driven by curiosity and guided by inspiration. She'd seen men as gifted as Baskins was, and women, too. People who would tap into another plane of cognizance that ran on parallels so close to that of their subjects that it was uncanny. She'd been fascinated with the process and with the results. But she'd never given thought to how the people being questioned felt. Until now. Until she was forced to feel how transparent she'd obviously become for Baskins. How flawed.

"This deep has turned rogue, hasn't he?" Baskins pressed. "Jesus. No wonder you and Judson are trying to save your asses on this one. You're managing a deep that's gone over, trailed him here and muscled your way into one of the hottest drug operations in Miami." He shook his head in disbelief. "One of the highest-stakes games being played out right now, and you guys cut yourself into the action backing a wild card. Are you being crazy, Piper, or are you just being a damn fool?''

Silverman stepped forward, letting the anger guide her, channeling it into something that would manifest itself in something less than physical violence. She poked a forefinger at the man's chest. "You're wrong, Roger. And if you don't keep out of this thing as you were *requested* to, I'm going to put a bug in Judson's ear to see if we can't make it something a little more permanent."

"Judson doesn't scare me."

"Well, maybe I can, Roger. Remember that bust you had in '88 involving the Harrington kid? I helped you work that one because the kid was making New York connections with some of his rich friends. You made your case against the Harrington kid down here. But you didn't exactly play by the rules, did you? You found a square peg and a round hole where you were expecting a square hole, so you found a bigger hammer and made the case stick. A few words in the right places might reopen that case, you know, and maybe make the agency reconsider your last few evaluations. You might end up with some spot less desirable than the Miami area. If you didn't end up drawing unemployment somewhere."

"You wouldn't . . ."

"I would," she asserted with venom. "You push me, Roger, I push back harder. That's one thing you should know about me. And I don't stop pushing once I start." She waited, letting it sink in, seeing the flaring nostrils signaling the man's restrained anger. "I also stand beside the people who stand by me because I don't like staring over my shoulder all the time. Do we understand each other?"

"I never thought I'd see this side of you, kid."

"I never thought I'd see the day you tried cutting corners with me, Roger. A few minutes ago you were the one putting down all the competition between the different departments, yet now you seem to be the one reaching for the scum.''

"I'm not reaching, kid. There's plenty of cesspool to go around for everybody. You and Judson can keep this deep for yourselves if you think you can, but you remember there's going to be a lot of players in this game once things start going wrong.''

There already are, Silverman thought. But she didn't say anything.

"I didn't mean to step on your toes, Piper. But just the same, if I'd known how fucked your operation was, I'd have taken some vacation about now and kept myself clear of it. When it blows up, you and Judson are going to get more ink than you can stand. I don't think I'll feel as regretful for you now as I would have before we had this talk.''

She watched Baskins walk away, feeling the loneliness and insecurity she'd experienced since Toronto scratch at her soul like fingernails against a blackboard of guilt.

5

Mack Bolan stayed well within the fringe reaches of the grounds surrounding the private beach house. The light rain had transmuted into a soft mist that blew in from the sea, bringing a briny smell with it. Everything still dripped, and with the humidity what it was, the big warrior knew the area wouldn't even start drying out for hours. That made it even easier to glide toward his objective like the shadow he resembled, because the few branches the landscapers left on the manicured grounds were too damp to snap out in warning.

Togged out in the nightsuit, with his features tiger striped by blackface, he knew he would be almost impossible to separate from the backdrop of the palms. Even by the men who would be posted around the perimeters by Hunsaker.

He moved under a palm, melding with it as he reached for the small high-powered binoculars at his waist. Cold rain fell across his shoulders and tightened the skin briefly before he put it out of his mind. He focused on the nearest lighted window, searching for details.

The woman had told him everything she knew about Hunsaker before he'd released her, revealing a tale that was both simplistic and twisted. But the bottom line was opportunity and greed, underscoring a profit margin that had been soaring for months.

Elongated shadows moved within the cabin, stuttering across the closed blinds as Bolan mentally set up the hard probe.

Hunsaker was a talented organizer with all the right connections. As Ronny Hunsaker, he was a big contributor to the Miami community's social improvement projects as well as a public backer of a harsh legal penalty against drug smugglers and street dealers. Yet as Ronald J. Hunsaker, he was a gifted attorney often found on retainer for a handful of the larger criminals trolling Miami's beaches. The woman hadn't hesitated to drop names after Bolan convinced her she wasn't going to be harmed. Some of those names belonged to people the Executioner had been expecting his raids to turn up. Ronny Hunsaker, good old boy lawyer and cocaine speculator, hadn't even been in the picture until the woman put him there.

Shadows drifted across the blinds again, more forcefully this time. Bolan tracked the movement, estimating where his quarry might show up next. He swept his view across the virgin white surface of the beach house, pausing at a large plate-glass window overlooking the sea and most likely offering a spectacular view of a sunrise that was only a handful of hours away.

The view, the beach house and the sixty-foot yacht moored at a private dock cost a lot of money. According to the woman, Hunsaker'd had all of it before moving onto the drug scene. Now, she assumed, it was just easier to afford the upkeep. She said Duncan had hired people to backtrack the attorney at different times and had found out about the beach house. Duncan had been hoping to turn up something he could use to blackmail Hunsaker, but hadn't managed to come up with anything. Hunsaker kept a quiet operation and a smooth one, with plenty of insurance to see that he was neither implicated nor troubled by the people he dealt with.

A man stepped into view on the other side of the plate glass window. He was dressed in a white turtleneck, white duck pants and a dark blue blazer. The blond hair had just the right amount of gray in it to be photogenic and still not add ten years to the guy's age. The closing curtains blurred away the angry look filling the tanned face.

Bolan had seen enough to convince him the man was Hunsaker. He put the binoculars away and moved on, letting instinct and experience lead off on a tangent that would put him on a collision course with the beach house.

His mind searched out for possibilities and connections as he moved, trying to separate the events of Hunsaker's story from the trouble he'd seen at the marina. And he was sure they were separate, leaving him with even more of a puzzle than either situation would have alone.

He brushed a wet leaf from his face slowly, searching for Hunsaker's bodyguards with more than just his eyes and ears. Combat senses, honed in lush and verdant jungles half a world away, had proved invaluable in his quest through the concrete hunting grounds his targets thrived in now.

Hunsaker had been the broker and the chairman over the latest cocaine pipeline to hit Miami's beaches and spread a consistently good supply northward in increasing quantity. It had all come together, the woman had said, when Hunsaker had defended some high-ranking members of the Medellin cartel the previous October. The case had been built for almost a year by a local DEA man named Baskins, and had gone to court before a jury by an assistant DA with ten years' trial experience. It should have been a go, because the DEA had pushers who were willing to roll over on the Colombians for reduced sentences. Then Ronald J. Hunsaker took over as defense attorney and busted the case all to hell. There were unconfirmed rumors that Hunsaker mediated deals between the witnesses and the Colombians for cash and threats. Another rumor suggested that Hunsaker had negotiated a contract with a local wiseguy that removed the two dealers who wouldn't reach for the cash. Maybe the cops were in on it, as well, guys whom Hunsaker had helped out on occasion and still owed him. But everything was just rumor and suspicion, at least as far as a court of law was concerned. When a vice detective had made some comments implicating Hunsaker in the newspapers, he had successfully sued, and it ultimately cost the detective his job. And in the meantime, he'd set himself up with the Colombians as a contractor. Hunsaker arranged deals for shipments, then used his contacts within the drug networks he had been defending for years, setting up buys and deliveries without even being near the operation. He knew the Miami area extensively, knew who could be trusted to move the product honestly and craftily. As a defense lawyer, Hunsaker had turned out to be a hell of a talent scout for the Colombian producers. He'd come up with a deal sweet enough to interest everyone involved.

As a result the past few months had seen Ronny Hunsaker start taking grave losses in the popularity polls he had at one time dominated.

But Bolan figured the man wasn't bothered by that loss at all. Judging from the continued success of the system Hunsaker had put into play, the lawyer was too busy building an empire to aspire to any public awards. And the money continued to spill in, flooding the pockets of corrupt judges and cops whenever the need arose, a green frosting overlaying the white snow that was showering the sun-dappled beaches. Like the cocaine, there was plenty of it to go around. When it needed to.

The operation had spread like a hydra, with tentacles reaching everywhere. Only, unlike that mythical sea monster, the hydra Bolan hunted had only one head.

And the Executioner had arrived, all set to remove it.

Afterward the host body would die a little more each day as the system fell into dysfunction and the justice system was encouraged to hold sway again in this corner of the world. Hopefully it would bear fruit. Even if only for a little while.

It was that hope and dream that pushed Bolan through his solitary life. Justice worked. Most of the time. Every now and then, though, you had to give it a shove. And the Executioner didn't mind stepping forward to do the job.

Radio static crackled and popped to his left, then became quickly muted.

Bolan froze, becoming one with the bush he crouched behind. His hand wrapped around the hilt of the Ka-bar sheathed in his left boot, slid it free. The mat finish of the blade gleamed dully for just an instant before he masked it in the shadow of his body. He strained his hearing, focusing on the faint radio projection.

Three cars were parked out in front of the beach house. Bolan had the Mercedes pegged as Hunsaker's, but guessed the remaining two belonged to the men the attorney had called out to watch over him while he finished up last-minute business.

Bolan shifted his weight forward, resting it on the balls of his toes, ready to uncoil at a second's notice. If he had to, he'd use the silenced Beretta to take the man out. But the knife meant close work, and he wanted to control the falling body if at all possible.

The guard walked tall and unafraid through the cloistered palms, carrying a MAC-10 in one hand and a walkie-talkie in the other. He was big and blocky, as though he'd been formed of rough-cut 4X4 timbers and had the flesh draped on later. He wore jeans, a light windbreaker and a baseball cap. Lifting the walkie-talkie, he spoke into it briefly, then clipped it at his belt, wrapping his arm back through the strap of the MAC-10.

When he drew even with the warrior's position, Bolan sprang forward, shoving the Ka-bar into the guard's throat as he grabbed a fistful of the man's shirt. The guard made a feeble grab for the trigger of the MAC-10, staring into Bolan's eyes in openmouthed astonishment. Then died. Silently.

Struggling with the man's weight, the Executioner pulled the corpse from view and covered it as best as he could with the surrounding foliage. He left the walkie-talkie on the dead man after shutting it off, knowing that the risk of carrying it and having it suddenly come to life and reveal his position far outweighed the benefit of the Intelligence he might gain concerning the other guards. He cleaned the knife carefully on the corpse's pants leg, then dropped it back in its sheath.

Some of the men would be inside the beach house. Hunsaker would have it no other way. The man was out of his depth and was smart enough to know it. But there was nowhere for the attorney to turn for help because he wouldn't know exactly what the investigation at the marina had turned up.

Bolan could feel the passage of time, too, because he was just as unaware how much the law enforcement people had been able to find out. He'd been lucky. The woman he'd confiscated from the police had been intelligent and curious. Most of the people left aboard the yacht would be waiting on attorneys or hoping to cut deals with the DA's office. That would serve to buy some time, but how much, he didn't know. Everybody had seemed involved with the bust tonight.

An image of the female DEA agent's face as she reached for the dead biker flickered through his mind. There was something else about the operation that was off, as well. Something that had intersected the violence at the marina but hadn't truly been a part of it. How much time would that add or subtract?

He moved quietly, taking the baseball cap from the dead man and closing his circle.

At least two men inside, armed as the outside guard had been, and a few more outside. Not many, he was sure, because Hunsaker wouldn't want to draw attention to his activities at the moment.

Unleathering the 93-R, he sprinted the remaining distance to the back of the beach house, knowing he would be highly visible once he reached those white walls. The numbers kept pace with him, dropping through his mind as he plowed through the unsure sand.

Autofire burst the silence, chopping into the wet sand with meaty smacks.

Bolan dropped, skidding behind a thick palm tree as he reached into the military webbing at his waist. His fingers found the spherical outline of a MISAR grenade as he searched for the shooter.

Hoarse shouts pealed from the beach house, and the lights died in the different rooms unevenly one by one.

Leaves and branches dropped from the tree, showering Bolan's shoulders as he raised himself up long enough to hurl the grenade in the direction of the muzzle-flashes. He shielded his eyes from the resulting flash, taking time to glance at the beach house.

The explosion rocketed through the palms, giving vent to even more shouts from the dwelling.

Glancing back in the direction he'd thrown the MISAR, the Executioner saw the crumpled outlines of a corpse against the whiteness of the sand. Patches of flame clung to the clothing.

Satisfied the man was dead, Bolan gave the immediate area a quick recon, tracking the 9 mm in his hand as he reached for another grenade. Nothing moved. Getting to his feet, he hurled the smoker through the plate glass window with enough force to spin it past the heavy curtains and left his position just as a hail of bullets thunked into the tree trunk where he'd been standing.

He triggered a 3-round burst at the plate glass window, focusing on the muzzle-flashes. Broken glass spun like diamond chips from the window. The automatic weapon disappeared back inside immediately.

Someone yelled, "Grenade!" Then there was the muffled whump of the smoker's explosion.

Slamming into the back of the house, Bolan shot the door lock out then kicked the door open. The bolts shrilled as they ripped free of the door frame.

Sporadic gunfire from the front of the beach house spilled more glass from the shattered window. "Stop shooting till you find out where the bastard is!" a man's voice yelled.

"I can't get Mike or Louis on the radio," another voice announced. "They must've already took them out."

Bolan followed the door inside, the tiredness forgotten as he anted up for the game. He traded the Beretta for the high-powered velocity of the Desert Eagle.

Smoke trailed from the forward rooms, climbing snake-like for the stucco ceiling, a lighter, moving darkness against the night trapped inside the beach house. An arm emerged out of the smoke, pursued by a choking voice and another arm cradling a MAC-10.

Dropping the heavy .44 into target acquisition, Bolan waited till he could make out the man's features, not wanting to take out Hunsaker by accident. He'd invested too much time in tracking the man down to lose him so quickly. Somebody like the attorney would more than likely keep records of the things he was involved in to make sure no one cut him out of his fair share. And as protection from those he used as well as from those who found a use for his services.

The big Magnum boomed in the narrow confines of the hallway, dimming the warrior's hearing for a time. The bearded man holding the MAC-10 staggered backward as the muzzle raked autofire into the wall. White plaster dust stained the smoke and settled on the corpse slumped against the wall.

The Executioner swung around the corner of the hallway, covering the immediate area with the Desert Eagle. Flickering images from a television screen in the living room threw wavering shadows over the ceramic walls of the kitchen separating him from the other room.

"There's somebody in the house, Mr. Hunsaker," a man said.

His ears still ringing from the exchange of shots inside the beach house, Bolan searched for the speaker, his eyes burning from the smoke residue and cordite.

A whirl of movement defined a shape at the doorway leading to the living room only an instant before autofire ripped through the hollow silence in the house and bullets reduced the refrigerator in front of Bolan to white enameled junk.

Recoiling from the autofire, the Executioner waited till the shooter exhausted his clip, then stepped back around the doorway, aiming at a spot on the left wall that he judged to be chest high. The .44 jumped in his hands as he squeezed out the remaining rounds of the clip, keeping them confined to an area he could have covered with a piece of typing paper.

A heavy bulk sprawled forward and lay still.

After he dropped the empty magazine to the tiled floor, Bolan slammed a fresh one home, snapping the slide to chamber the first round.

He paused to listen, to let his senses and instinct inform him of the next move he needed to make. He inched forward, letting the Desert Eagle point the way.

Stepping over the dead man sprawled on the expensive shag carpet, he found the living room empty and the front door waving in the breeze. The telephone on the end of a small rolltop desk rang, piercing the cotton that filled his ears. Disregarding it, he hurried over to the door and glanced out over the manicured landscaping that had converted so easily to a battle zone. He felt a fleeting moment of regret as he observed the carnage left by the grenade, reflecting that this place of beauty would never hold the same memories for anyone on the beach again, knowing it would serve as a house of horrors for a time before the rumors grew and the pain passed. Someone had gone to a lot of trouble to make this section of the beachfront resemble a garden of Eden, then got a bad break when he made a deal with a snake like Hunsaker.

A moving flash of white among the palms flared into the periphery of Bolan's vision. He realized the attorney hadn't chosen a car or the yacht for his escape.

Propelling himself away from the door, he leaped off the wooden porch and threw himself into pursuit.

The palm trees became a maze once he hit the foliage line. Branches whipped at him, stinging his face. He searched for the whiteness of the man's clothing, his hearing still blunted and almost useless from the gunfire and against the noises he made himself. Where? The man couldn't get away.

The flatness of the ground inclined sharply and without warning. He almost fell, dragging his free hand across the wet sand as he struggled to maintain his balance. There was a sharp crack, and something clipped a branch from the brush in front of him.

He let himself go with the pull of gravity. His chest hit the wet sand as both hands locked on the Desert Eagle in front of him. Letting his breath out slowly, ignoring the anxious thumping of his heart as his lungs demanded more oxygen, he scanned the dark hill, trying to find Hunsaker's silhouette against the palms and brush. Was the man waiting, or had it only been a delaying shot that had come uncomfortably close?

He rolled, coming to a rest behind a palm trunk as he forced himself to his feet. No movement followed him. Hunsaker was still running.

He stumbled over a gnarled root as he clambered to the top of the incline. When he reached the crest, he dropped to one knee and swept his eyes and the muzzle of the Desert Eagle across the down slope.

The landscaping ended here, and a smattering of palm trees fought cypress trees for territorial rights.

The air felt cool, biting as he drew it in.

Hunsaker was halfway down, half running and half sliding, heading toward a tilted, weather-gray building. Dulled ruby reflections gleamed from the taillights of a vehicle parked inside.

Bolan broke cover, breaking into a zigzag that carried him safely down the treacherous slope, closing the distance between himself and the attorney, knowing he would be too late to keep Hunsaker from getting inside the building.

Without warning, operating on some instinctive sense, Hunsaker turned for an instant and thrust the barrel of his pistol in his pursuer's direction.

The Executioner followed the line of movement, sprawling forward in an effort to get below the wildly placed shots. The bullets smacked into the wet ground and bit into the trees. The Desert Eagle was out before him, tracking the fleeing man's chest. His finger hovered a heartbeat over death.

Then he heard the dry snap of Hunsaker's revolver as it pumped empty.

Rising to his feet, Bolan saw his quarry toss the pistol to one side and swing himself around the corner of the build-

ing. He ran, half stumbling down the incline as he took too-
big steps and hit the loose surface in jarring thumps.

The motor of the hidden vehicle caught just as the Executioner gained level ground. A pulsebeat later, a 4X4 Ram
Charger exploded through the loosely hinged double doors
with a snarling of its powerful engine.

Coming to a stop, Bolan swiveled the big .44 up to steady
his hands in a Weaver's grip. He sighted, released his breath
halfway and held his aim.

The immense 4X4 inscribed a quarter circle in the loose
turf, sending sand showers over the nearby foliage. The rpm
increased as it rocked to an unsteady halt, squarely facing
Bolan. Hunsaker's shadow jerked inside the cab, fighting
for control of the wheel.

Bolan squeezed the trigger, aiming for the tires as the big
metal monster bore down on him, feeling the Magnum buck
in his hands as he stood his ground. Even if he punctured the
radiator, the 4X4 wouldn't stop. There would be enough life
left in the vehicle to take it at least to the highway long minutes ahead of the Executioner, making escape possible if not
probable.

Finishing off the magazine as the Ram Charger fish-
tailed toward him, Bolan dived to one side, pushing off the
truck's hood as he arced his body for distance. Both front
tires had deflated as a result of his marksmanship in the uncertain moonlight, but would it be enough?

He hit the ground on his back, grateful for the sand's
cushioning effect, and rolled to his feet as the 4X4 charged
into the underbrush to slam into a broad-based palm tree.
He slid a fresh magazine into the butt of the Desert Eagle as
he moved forward.

The hiss of the vehicle's smashed radiator filled the night
air, exciting the crickets and night birds. One of the front
wheels was off the ground and spun lazily.

Following the .44's lead, Bolan stepped to the side of the Ram Charger, hoping Hunsaker was still alive. Things on the Miami end of the operation were getting too hot to let him remain operative in the area. Yet he couldn't be sure the new pipeline from Colombia would be effectively closed down without talking to the attorney first. He'd taken some big steps in that direction tonight, and he wasn't going to remove himself from the picture till he could be sure.

Hunsaker was moaning, slumped over the steering wheel. A cut over one eye was leaking slow drops of dark blood, staining the white turtleneck in patterns that differed from the mud and brush stains accumulated there.

The door was jammed from the impact, and Bolan had to yank on it twice to open it. Reluctantly it gave with a shrill screech that mingled with the sputtering of the dying radiator.

Bolan nudged the attorney with the heated barrel of the Desert Eagle. "Out of the truck, Hunsaker. Hands behind your head. You may not remember all the details, but you've associated with the law long enough that some of it should have rubbed off."

Hunsaker moaned, refusing to move, wrapping his fingers around the steering wheel. "Who are you?" he asked through bloody lips.

Bolan didn't answer, reaching into the depth of the oversize cab to grasp the attorney by the lapels of his blazer. He yanked, spilling the man to the ground.

Hunsaker glared up at him, the blond hair in wild disarray. "You don't know who you're messing with, guy. I've got protection. You can't get away with this shit with me."

Dropping the Desert Eagle into target acquisition between the man's eyes, Bolan said, "Do you think your protection is going to do you any good if I pull this trigger? Do you feel protected now?"

Hunsaker's eyes widened. "You wouldn't dare."

"This isn't the world you're accustomed to dealing with, Hunsaker," Bolan said. "You don't make deals here and play with lives without being touched. This world we're locked in now was created from the dregs of emotions, the baser instincts of survival and jealousy and greed. Everything in this world spins on the point of a knife, and no one passes through it without shedding blood at one time or another. You've been lucky until now. You've set yourself up nicely in this operation, taking your cut off the top without getting your hands dirty doing any of the actual work. Maybe you viewed what you were doing as being a broker, rationalized so that none of the dirt clung to you while you made your deals between the Colombians and the people you knew in the drug business. To me, you're a pimp. Nothing more. And maybe something less, in light of the way you've prostituted the legal system to make it work for you."

Hunsaker lifted his hands before him, holding his wrists together. "If you're a cop, you have to take me in."

The bore of the Magnum never wavered in Bolan's hand. "I'm not a cop, Hunsaker. I'm the kind of justice you can't buy off or intimidate or simply escape from through legal loopholes. We're living in the world *you* chose to operate in, and you don't find loopholes here. Justice in this world is retribution, and to even survive against the odds, that justice has to be unswerving and disciplined, unanswerable to anyone."

"You're crazy."

Bolan shook his head and sighed. "Get up."

Hunsaker started to stand.

Bolan tapped the attorney painfully on the head. "Hands behind your neck."

Hunsaker complied, and all the while he kept staring at the pistol. Perspiration streamed down his face, but he didn't seem to notice.

"Let's go."

"Where?"

"Back to the beach house."

"Why?"

Bolan gave the man a grim smile. "To cut a deal, Hunsaker. That's what you're waiting for, isn't it?"

The attorney relaxed a little, his shoulders hanging pensively as if afraid he was being tricked. "I thought there weren't going to be any deals."

"You've organized a big operation here, Ronny, and I aim to dismantle it to the point that it can't be started up again so readily. I figure you're about the best man available to help me with the job. You're the kind of guy who would keep notes on the deals he's made and who he's made them with. As insurance. I want to see what your bottom-line net worth is. Then we can negotiate."

A hesitant smile flirted with Hunsaker's puffy lips. "I've got plenty of notes, mister, and I'd cut a deal with the Devil himself if I had to."

"You might have gotten a better offer from him. All he'd have wanted is your soul, and you don't seem to have much use for that. I deal in flesh and blood."

6

"Oh, Jesus," Hunsaker said in a whisper-thin voice. He froze in the doorway, staring at the dead body sprawled on the carpet.

Bolan settled the muzzle of the Desert Eagle between the attorney's shoulders and said, "Move." Following his captive into the beach house living room, he looked searchingly around, making sure the four men he'd taken out accounted for all of the security team Hunsaker had summoned to his defense. Nothing moved under the pall of death that hovered over the room.

Hunsaker stumbled across the carpet, his eyes focused on the corpse.

Now that the ebb of action had died away and the tension had been eased out of his system by the walk back to the beach house, Bolan could feel the fatigue chafing at his awareness. He'd accomplished a lot in the last handful of hours, had succeeded in making a bigger strike against the cocaine pipeline than legal resources in the area would have been able to make for weeks and perhaps months. But there was still a lot to be done before he pulled himself out of the perimeter of the forces operating around Miami. He was satisfied the beach house had been built where it was for security as well as privacy. There was small chance of a police or sheriff's department being notified of the disturbance that had taken place.

The telephone rang again, visibly unsettling the attorney's nerves. His clasped hands behind his neck trembled.

On the third ring an answering machine picked up the call. "You've called me on my private line," Hunsaker's recorded voice said, "so it had better be damn well important. Make it short. And make it sweet." A beep followed.

"C'mon, Ronny, pick up the damn phone. You're the one who called in the first place and got me out of bed tonight. I don't need this kind of shit while I'm recovering from this hernia operation." The man's voice paused, waiting expectantly, then hurried on. "You're an asshole, Ronny, you know that? I unloaded the stocks we were talking about, and cut a damn fine deal for you on such a quick turnover, too. You can thank me by sending me a bonus. I've already got the moneys converted, and it'll be waiting for you in that Nassau bank we discussed. Hope this little number you've developed the hots for is worth it." The line clicked dead.

"Who?" Bolan asked.

Hunsaker's pasty white face seemed to dissolve into a featureless, uncertain mass.

Keeping the sharp distaste he felt for the man from his expression, Bolan said, "You cover a lot of corners when you start cutting them, Ronny."

The attorney smiled nervously, as if unsure how to take the statement.

"Where's the information you promised me?"

"I'll have to use the computer on the desk to access my files from home," Hunsaker said.

"Let's go."

Hunsaker bit his lip and looked away for a moment, then looked back. "Look, I don't know who you are or why the hell you're even doing this. And I don't want to know. So how do I know you're not scamming me?"

Bolan didn't reply. His guts churned from having to even deal with the man. And he wouldn't have if the stakes involved didn't warrant it. But if he was going to dismantle the pipeline, he needed the blueprints.

"It would be real easy for you to tell me that you'll let me go after I give you what you want, then go ahead and pull that trigger."

Bolan saw the desperation welling up in the man's eyes now, sensed that Hunsaker was hovering close to the breaking point. Death was too much a part of the room now, and he knew the man could see impending violence in every move he made. "You're right," he said as honestly as he could. "It would be very easy to pull the trigger, easier than letting you walk away from here once you get me the information. But that just goes to show you, Ronny, if you even get close to it, the paranoia of the world you've been dealing with will infect you. I won't kill you because I said I won't. My word means something."

"Not to me, it doesn't."

Flashing the attorney a shark's grin, Bolan said, "It does now, counselor, because it's the only thing that's keeping you alive at the moment."

"I have money. A lot of it. Can't we make some kind of deal?"

"We are making a deal."

Hunsaker pointed at the recording machine. "My broker was talking about a lot of money just now, and it can be yours if you say the word."

"Meaning you would find me more believable if you could find the smallest amount of corruption in me? Isn't that contradictory?"

Hunsaker licked his lips and looked torn between loyalties.

"I'm offering you the only deal you're going to get, Hunsaker," Bolan said in a graveyard voice. "And you're not going to get anywhere by wasting my time. I'm on a tight schedule, and that little jaunt through the forest ate up a lot of minutes.''

"I'll need to put my hands down to operate the keyboard.''

"As long as you do it slowly, we won't have any problems.''

Hunsaker nodded and seated himself behind the desk.

Bolan watched him closely, keeping the Desert Eagle within easy sight of the man.

Lifting the phone, the attorney settled it on a modem, then flicked the keyboard and monitor to quiet green life. The tapping of the keys sounded hollow and loud in the room.

Bolan could still smell the scent of cordite in the air as images of the carnage around him swirled in his memory indelibly. How many hardsites had he fought his way through in his wars against the Mafia and the terrorists? He couldn't begin to imagine the number. And no matter what, it never became truly comfortable. War was a skill, and being a warrior was a profession, though it seemed less honorable in modern times than it had been centuries ago.

He stared into the depths of the emerald screen over Hunsaker's shoulder, gleaning information from the lines that continually scrolled upward. Many of the names were familiar; some he'd turned up since arriving in Miami, and others he'd come down armed with.

"Satisfied?'' the attorney asked.

"Yeah. As soon as I get a printout.''

Hunsaker made a couple of entries on the keyboard, and the printer at the side of the desk began clattering in quick response.

"Now can I get out of here?'' Hunsaker asked.

"After we talk,'' Bolan replied.

"About what? Everything you want to know is on here, including deals that I set up to take place weeks from now.

You've even got the names of the contacts I developed in Bogota, if it will do you any good."

"It will."

Hunsaker looked as if he clearly didn't believe him but didn't care to dispute the statement.

Bolan didn't enlighten the man. "Tell me about the Death's Enforcers."

"I don't know much."

"Let me be the judge of that."

Hunsaker wiped a sleeve nervously along his mouth. "They're a biker gang from Toronto. They set up a deal with Duncan."

"How much product was involved?"

"Almost ten million dollars' worth."

"How did you get involved with bikers from Toronto, Ronny? Until lately you've only been handling the local business and letting others take care of the transportation risks."

Hunsaker looked as though he was searching for a rock to crawl under.

The printer clattered away. "Clock's ticking, counselor," Bolan prodded in a quiet voice.

Hunsaker swallowed hard, eyes focusing briefly on the muzzle of the .44, then shifting back to Bolan. The Executioner kept his own features as immobile and unforgiving as the barrel of the Desert Eagle.

"It was family action from Toronto," he said in defeated tones.

"What family?"

"Jesus, do you know what you're asking? It's one thing to roll over on the lowlifes I've been working through and the Colombians, who don't have much reach outside Florida, but you're talking about people who can have you hit anywhere in the United States."

Bolan remained silent, wearing the man down with an icy stare. Hunsaker gritted his teeth and let his breath hiss out. "It was the Corsini Family. They're setting up a deal with some heavy internationals in Toronto and needed a big score to open negotiations. A biker captain set up the deal through the local chapter of Outlaws and passed it on to Duncan. Jesus, is that what this is all about? Did someone tumble to the deal because of the Canadian angle? I told Duncan it sounded too good, that things would be too spread out to cover effectively, but he wouldn't listen. He just kept on saying how much . . ."

"Duncan's dead," Bolan reminded the attorney, shifting the pistol to bring the man's eyes back on a line with it.

"Yeah. I know."

"So you don't know what the Death's Enforcers members were going to do with the cocaine?"

"Duncan knew something about it. At least he pretended as though he did to me. Said something about the biker captain being considered for membership in the Corsini Family and needing to square the deal to make his bones."

As the printer fell silent, Bolan turned that over in his mind, poking at the thought tentatively. Promotion from a Mafia-sponsored biker gang happened rarely. And only then to individuals who proved able and competent, and willing to drop the rough image of the biker for the flashy life-style the Mafia demanded of its elite members. The memory of Special Agent Piper Silverman of the DEA jarred into his thoughts with a suddenness that almost distracted him. He saw the pain of the fear of discovery etched into her face as he helped her turn the dead biker over. A thin thread of logic spun itself into a complex web of possibilities as he confronted the new information and matched it against the questions that had surfaced at the marina.

"Who were the internationals?" Bolan asked.

"I don't know. It wasn't important. The only thing Duncan was interested in was whether the bikers could come up with the cash."

"Did they?"

"I don't know. Duncan was working that deal tonight, when the cops took the *Swift Tiger*."

"What names did Duncan mention?"

"I think the Death's Enforcers leader's name was Thornton but I'm not sure. Duncan handled his own deals after fronting me a percentage of the cash involved. If he burned, he was to burn on his own and he knew that."

What other stakes were involved in the game that had been played out at the marina? Bolan ran it through his mind again, convinced that more than just the takedown of Duncan had been involved. It had been a suck. From start to finish. But how many different ways was the suck supposed to work, and how many different ways had it failed? Cops were dead. A biker was dead. The prime catch on the dealers' side was dead by the Executioner's own hand. His mind flashed a vivid image of the female agent's face again. Somewhere in the chaos of crime and crime busters on the scene was someone Silverman had feared for.

"You're not going to let me go, are you?" Hunsaker asked.

"Letting you go wasn't part of the deal," Bolan said as he walked around the printer stand to take up the printed sheets. "The deal was that you would live."

"You call going to prison letting me live?" Exasperation and fear fought for control of the attorney's face. "How the hell do you expect me to live with the animals that are locked up in those cages?"

"Maybe you can cut deals inside those concrete walls, counselor. You've certainly learned how to deal with the people you'll be sharing cells with. Of course, it's going to be different now that you don't have the upper hand and can't wave their futures before them like you held a controlling interest.'' Bolan placed the .44 aside as he pulled the paper from the printer. ''Shut down the computer and let's go.''

''You said you weren't a cop.''

''I'm not, but that doesn't mean I can't turn you in.''

''This is crazy. We had a deal.''

''And I mean to keep it.'' Feeling wearied by the whine in the man's voice, Bolan folded the perforated sheets, skimming across the information contained in the neatly printed lines.

Without warning, Hunsaker kicked out, knocking the printer stand over, and leaped from his chair.

Bolan grabbed the man's blazer, then felt it skate freely through his fingertips as the heavy equipment collided painfully against his shins. He cleared the printer and stand out of his way, reaching for the Desert Eagle.

The attorney skidded across the desk and made a rolling dive for the MAC-10 in the dead man's hands. He brought it up already firing. A ragged line of bullets tore holes in the ceiling, pouring sheetrock dust down in streaming spirals.

Bolan fired from the waist as the autofire raked toward him. The powerful and deadly projectile caught Hunsaker in the upper chest and flung him backward.

Trying to speak, Hunsaker reached for the MAC-10 again, then died even as his fingers brushed against it.

Bolan gathered up the scattered papers, giving the attorney's body a final glance. He felt better about the closing argument the prosecution had been forced into than he would have if he'd turned the man over to local authorities. Maybe the families of the slain policemen who'd given their lives to close down Hunsaker's creation would sleep better when they found out how things had ended here in the beach house.

But had they really ended?

He made his way out of the dwelling, focusing his thoughts on the vague connections he'd turned up at the marina.

He tucked the printout inside the blacksuit as he faded into the palm trees and became part of the oppressive silence dominating the killground.

Part of the product Hunsaker had moved onto the scene was still freewheeling back toward Toronto. Grimly he faced the fact that he wasn't ready to let it go yet, not until he came to a more comprehensive overview. Gaining access to the information the DEA was privy to wouldn't be easy. But he felt confident the information he'd taken from Hunsaker would be enough of an ante to buy him a stake in the pot as the hand played out.

And he planned on figuring out at least some of the cards his opponents held in their hands before sitting in.

DRIZZLING RAIN STREAKED the phone booth windows as Bolan waited for the connection to be made. He shivered against the night chill, wishing he had time for breakfast, a shave, a bath and bed. In that order. But things were breaking too fast, and he was playing catch-up. The Death's Enforcers members could be anywhere within a two-hundred-mile radius by now and still moving. That is, assuming they didn't try to make an aerial jaunt anytime soon.

"Hello?" Hal Brognola's voice sounded thick with the need for sleep.

Bolan grinned, feeling relaxed with the proximity he felt over the phone line to the head Fed. His connection with the government was an arm's-length alliance that functioned solely on a need-to-know basis. He was still considered a lone wolf by those who knew that he accepted operations of mutual interest through the Justice Department from time to time—a lone wolf with sporadic, temporary amnesty. In his chosen struggle the warrior had found true friendships, then found he had precious little time to pursue them. Even when he had time with close people like Brognola, impending disaster usually threw a shadow over the more human instincts that wanted to show. "Striker here. Can we talk?"

"Yes. Trouble?"

"Because I called you in the middle of the night, Hal? Sometimes when you come to the phone, I have to think hard to remember what you sound like when you're immediately lucid." Bolan watched the pink neon Vacancy sign fizzle on and off through the falling rain, then watched the headlights of a car that pulled onto the graveled parking area of the small motel, relaxing when the occupants seemed to take no notice of him.

"Where are you?"

"In Miami."

Brognola cleared his throat. "I hear things are getting pretty hot down that way right now."

"I put a chill on some of it, big guy."

"The new pipeline?"

"Yeah."

"I didn't know you were in town."

"Neither did a lot of other people, but they're going to know it soon."

"I hope you're not planning on sticking around down there."

"Originally I'd scammed this as a one-night hit-and-git mission. No hellzones until I at least felt like I was close to the primary target."

"Did you get close?"

"I closed the books on the pipeline engineer less than a half hour ago."

"That's an impressive piece of work, Striker. I hear a lot of people have been turning over rocks down there."

"I turned one over and let it land on the right people."

"So, what's the problem? Get the hell out of there and let the locals pick up the pieces. If it looks bad in a day or two, I'll put together a package through Justice that should hold up under the kind of scrutiny it's likely to get at that end of the world, and you can jump back in the middle. If that's what you want."

"I've got a handle on the domestic side of the water, Hal, and the target's been terminated."

"Then get back to the Farm for a brief R and R. I've got some stuff lined up that I've been wanting you to take a look at, anyway. Some heat is building up around the globe with Japanese interests here and abroad."

"We'll talk when I get back in Wonderland, Hal. If there's enough there, we'll see. There's too much to do here for me to just sit back and kick up my heels while we wait to see if a few maybes come through."

"I know how you feel, Striker." Brognola sighed. "So, what's happened down there in fun city?"

"The focus has broadened," Bolan said. A layer of fatigue, even more noticeable than the weight of the soaked trench coat, seemed to drape over him. He went on, summarizing the bust at the marina and the information about the Corsini Family and the Death's Enforcers gang in Toronto. Next he outlined the rumor about the biker captain who was supposed to be promoted into the ranks of the Mafia family, then fleshed it out with the distress he'd seen on Piper Silverman's face.

"So you figure the DEA has a ringer planted in the ranks of the Death's Enforcers?"

"Or they've got an informer in there. Either way, things went down wrong at the marina, Hal, and the guy has to know it. If he's an informer, I want to string along and make sure he stays turned in the right direction."

"And if he's undercover..."

"I'll do what I can to protect him."

"This isn't any of your affair, Striker. The DEA is filled with big boys and girls, people who are trained to take care of themselves."

"It's just a gut feeling, Hal. Something's screwy with the whole operation, but I can't put my finger on it. If the Toronto people are setting up buys from the Colombians, I want to nip that in the bud."

"You think they're the internationals Hunsaker mentioned?"

"It's a possibility."

"I can't provide you a cover, Striker. At least not without a running start and a guess at what kind of scope we're dealing with here. You're already talking about covering the whole eastern seaboard."

"I just need some Intel, Hal. I have the feeling it is going to play itself out on the streets, and unless you can manufacture a cover identity that's bulletproof, it's not going to do me much good. Plus I figure I can buy my own way in the enforcement machine backing the Death's Enforcers guy if I have to. I plan to be the joker in the deck in whatever game the DEA is running and stay loose. I'll make my own calls because it looks like whoever they've got heading this thing up is maintaining too much of a distance from their guy. I don't intend to stay back that far."

"What do you need?"

"I'm familiar with the Corsini Family, but I want whatever you can dig up on them."

"I'll give Leo a call. He should be able to give me some quick poop on them. Seems to me that I remember the Corsinis as a young branch of the Mafia just taking over in a big way in Canada."

"I'll also need some Intel on the out-of-state federal people that are involved down here. Special Agent Piper Silverman and her boss, a guy name Judson, but I don't know if that's his first name or last."

"I'll see what I can do, guy, but I'm not giving any promises."

"I wasn't expecting any."

"Yeah, well, this kind of operation usually moves so deep in the shadows that you don't get a whisper of it till it's over."

"There are people down here who are going to be talking about it now."

"I hear you. How am I going to get in touch with you?"

"I'll call."

"Okay. Give me at least an hour."

"You'll have that, Hal. I've got another connection or two to try to arrange myself. Like I said, I don't intend to cool my heels on this one."

"Turning the heat up down there?"

"It's blazing hellfire right now. I'm just waiting for a few of the enforcement teams to pick up the smell of smoke. I'm going to lie low for a little bit and try to find somebody who'll recognize a brief flag of truce."

"I wouldn't be overly zealous about that, Striker. Not if all those drug squad hot dogs are nosing around the area. Interagency cooperation isn't their strong suit."

"I've experienced some of that already," Bolan remarked dryly. He said thanks and hung up, then moved out into the spitting rain. He sat behind the wheel of the rental car and felt the chill of the vinyl soak into him. Taking a plastic cup of coffee from the dashboard, he removed the lid and downed the contents in a few long gulps, surprised the liquid had managed to withstand the night chill as well as it had. Or maybe it was the bleak thoughts filling his head that made him susceptible to the spring weather.

He tried to fit himself into the minds of the other players in the unnamed game in which he'd become an unknowing participant. From what he had seen at the marina, their plans hadn't been too well thought out, or the wrong players had been enlisted on the teams. Either way, ten million dollars' worth of cocaine was busy finding its way north— if he let it get that far. One way or another, even if he had to deliver the message himself, he wanted the buyers to know the Miami shop was out of business.

He started the car and engaged the transmission, sliding out onto the highway as he waited for the blower on the heater to kick into life. He was familiar with undercover officers' word for being undercover, and he idly speculated on whether or not the Death's Enforcers guy had any idea of just how "deep" he really was. Remembering the emotion that had shown on Piper Silverman's face, he reflected that at least one of the members of the deep team was all too aware of it.

In Bolan's mind, being deep was like being stranded on the wrong side of the DMZ with a BB gun as the only armament permitted. It didn't work unless you had a pat hand. And something told him the guy working the DEA end of things from the inside wasn't even being given a look at his cards.

"THAT BELASKO GUY didn't check out with the Coast Guard," Judson said in a harsh voice.

Silverman closed the door as she entered the small room the Miami PD had grudgingly loaned to them as a command post. She resisted the urge to make a scathing remark, because emotion was still running high in her from the confrontation with Baskins out in the hall. "What do you mean?"

Judson sat behind a folding table covered with phones, papers and maps. His eyes were bloodshot and almost matched the color of the crumpled tie to his left. "I mean the Coast Guard denies having anyone named Belasko on their payroll. Evidently this guy you turned up blew in from nowhere, then blew right back out again without anyone even checking his ID.''

The emphasis on the word *anyone* told Silverman that Judson had included her. At the top of the list. She resisted the impulse to ask her superior why he hadn't thought to ask for the man's ID. Shrugging out of her coat, she laid it across the back of a chair facing the table and put her purse on the seat. Too wound up to sit, she crossed the room to the coffee maker and poured herself a cup. She considered being polite and offering Judson a refill, then dismissed the idea at once, knowing the man would only view it as subservience. Judson hadn't wanted her on this operation from the outset, had he? He had been vocal about his doubts concerning her abilities, too. Maybe she'd even confirmed those doubts. Tears stung her eyes, and she blinked them away with effort.

She wished she could get out of the wet clothes. If Judson had allowed it, she would have dropped by the hotel room for a change of clothes. And maybe a bath, even a short one. God, the thought was appealing. Too appealing. Was it the thought of a long, hot bath, or was it the chance to be alone, to face her fears in private? She didn't know. Her hands trembled, and she had to use both to steady the coffee cup.

"No one made the guy?" she asked, meeting Judson's baleful stare.

"No." Judson shook his head irritably. He examined his empty coffee cup in frustration, then got up out of the folding metal chair to fill it himself. "The bastard was nervy, though. You got to give him that. Not only did he walk into the middle of our setup and give everybody the impression he belonged there, but he also wasted Duncan, then liberated a prisoner from one of the uniforms and boosted an unmarked car to take her away in.''

"And no one questioned him?''

Judson gave her a thin grin, one she had seen him wear only during intradepartmental politics when someone Frank Judson disliked was getting the short end of the stick. "Yeah, they questioned him. He dropped my name like we were buddies and kept pushing till he got what he wanted. This was one nervy son of a bitch, I'm telling you."

"Nobody has an idea of where Belasko came from?"

"Oh, they know how he got on the scene. One of the police snipers mentioned to his watch captain later that he wished I hadn't neglected to inform the SWAT teams of the man I had stationed on the roof because he almost took the guy out."

"The only DEA people on the scene were you and me and Baskins. We didn't have anyone on the roofs."

"The sniper got the general idea that Belasko was one of us from the way he palled around with you."

"Was he also the guy who got the idea to open fire before Thornton cleared the vicinity?"

Judson waved it away. "That's another topic."

"It's the one we need to be concerning ourselves with, Frank. I don't think it was just an itchy trigger finger that got that biker killed. I think the local cowboys were looking to pull off this bust by themselves. No matter who got hurt."

Reseating himself behind the folding table, Judson nodded. "Maybe. Maybe you're right, Piper. And maybe there's more to this Belasko character than meets the eye. What if it was Belasko who dropped the biker?"

"The shot came from the rooftops."

"Belasko was on the rooftops."

"It came from the SWAT guys, Frank. Are they trying to sell you on Belasko being the trigger man? Because if they are, it's only to pull their own asses out of a sling."

"Could be," Judson admitted. He sifted through the pile of papers before him.

Sipping her coffee, Silverman tried to absorb the warmth from her cup, holding both hands around it and trying not to shiver. She knew from experience that Judson was nudging the conversation in whatever direction he had chosen. The only defense she had managed to come up with during their association was to sit back and relax, waiting for whatever traps the man had set to snap at her.

"It also could be that Belasko is some kind of out-of-town talent. A report landed on Carruthers's desk almost two hours before the bust at the marina went sour concerning a handful of bodies in a local biker bar managed by the Outlaws."

Silverman shifted, feeling the wet leather of the shoulder harness chafe her uncomfortably. "What's the connection?"

"The guy who hit the bar matched the description we got of Belasko in a lot of ways."

"He's not the only big, dark guy in town."

Judson scowled his irritation, tapping a sheet of paper with a thick forefinger. "I know that, damn it. But these bikers were the Outlaws. Thornton made his deal for the cocaine through the Outlaws, remember?"

"And you think because their bar got hit tonight and Belasko turned up at the marina that the two things are somehow connected? That's a pretty thin assumption, don't you think?"

"Hell, yes, I think it's pretty thin. The problem is, that assumption shouldn't even exist. And to thicken it a little, the guy who hit the bar took a prisoner. Some hardass named Cullen, who, Carruthers tells me, has been known to do business with Duncan for the Outlaws. Neither the guy nor Cullen have turned up yet."

"Why is Carruthers being so helpful all of a sudden? When we first touched down here a few days ago, the man didn't even want to give us the time of day."

"I think he figures Belasko as belonging to us somehow and is hanging back to see if this blows up in our faces. Then he can step in to pick up the pieces. He's still pissed about the quantity of cocaine found aboard the *Swift Tiger*. Small busts don't count for shit in this town."

"Carruthers isn't hanging back very far on this one," Silverman said. In terse sentences, she briefed Judson on the conversation she'd had with Baskins out in the hallway, telling the man of the headhunting party Carruthers had unofficially set into motion.

"Thornton can take care of himself," Judson said when she was finished.

Silverman felt the anger flare inside her too quickly to sidestep it. "Ryan's been taking care of himself for a long time, Frank. Too damn long. You can't leave him on his own with this kind of pressure coming down."

Judson spoke slowly and deliberately. "I can and I will. We're so close to making this case I can smell it. I'm not going to back out now."

"Jesus Christ, Frank, will you look at what we're facing here? Ryan Thornton has been deep for almost eight months. That's too damn long. It would be even for somebody who hasn't been through everything he's been through."

"It was Thornton's decision to stay involved," Judson replied.

"He shouldn't even have been allowed the choice, Frank. Can you even imagine all the shit that has to be going through his mind right now? All the guilt?"

Judson remained silent, fastening an impenetrable stare on her.

She tried to return it, willing away the confusing haze of emotions that threatened to sweep her control away. But she broke eye contact because she couldn't stand the knowledge that lay in the hard glint of Judson's eyes.

"If Thornton is feeling any burdens of guilt about anything connected to this operation," Judson stated, "I have a clear conscience because I know I didn't put it there."

His words burrowed deep and hurt, just as she knew he meant them to. God, why couldn't she have been stronger—for Ryan, for herself? Why did the bad things only seem to happen to the best of people? And she knew she wasn't thinking of herself when she thought of those best of people. She fought back the tears, tasted them harsh and bitter across the roof of her mouth. How much did Judson really know and how much was he only guessing at? She didn't know, but every time she glanced at a mirror, she couldn't help but see it in her face, her eyes, in the way she carried herself.

"I want Belasko found," Judson went on, "and I want to know who he's working for. You're not going to tell me this bastard just wandered in off the street and accidentally found his way to the scene of a major DEA operation, snuffing an important vice prisoner during his stay. I won't buy that, and Carruthers isn't buying it, either. Only I know this guy isn't playing on our side of the field."

"What about Thornton?" she asked when she could trust her voice.

"He stays out there while we try to wrap this thing up in Toronto."

"He might not make it to Toronto."

"He'll make it," Judson said stubbornly. "Thornton's a resourceful man."

"Maybe he was once," Silverman said. "But you haven't sat through the last two meetings with him. Losing his family has taken a lot out of him."

"He wanted to stay in. It was his choice."

"Only because he didn't have anywhere else to go. He's hiding, Frank, hiding from himself and everything that's happened. There's no telling what he's thinking after nearly being shot down by the people he's supposed to be working with.''

"It's a tough racket, Silverman. Thornton knew that going in.''

"And what if he decides not to come out when the smoke clears, Frank?'' Her words hung heavy and still, and she wished she could take them back. But the image of the despondent figure Thornton had become in the last month weighed heavily in her mind, an image that truly gnawed at her conscience.

"You mean goes rogue?''

"Yes.''

"What makes you think that?''

Unable to hold the knowledge back and consider it wise to keep her own counsel anymore, Silverman said, "He missed the last meeting with me.''

Judson's interest was evident and immediate. "Any explanations?''

"No.''

"It may be nothing. He could have gotten tied up finalizing the cocaine deal for the Corsini Family and simply couldn't make it.''

"I know.'' She considered what would make Judson understand her feelings about what was happening. The man was too wrapped up in the end result of the operation he was heading up, too sure the end justified the means. If she did try to push to make her feelings known, wouldn't he only throw them back in her face and tell her they were only feelings? She felt torn, not knowing which way to go. Baskins's insight about Thornton had struck too deep and made her foundation seem shaky.

"The way I see it,'' Judson said, "we have more of a problem with who Belasko really is than with what Thornton might or might not do. Thornton's a good cop. Committed. You can't just wake up one day from a wild-assed dream and decide to shelve an attitude like that for a get-rich-quick scheme. Know what I mean?''

Silverman nodded, meeting the man's gaze but locking her thoughts in. Maybe someone like Ryan Thornton wouldn't set aside a life and career for a dream like that, but what if he was chased screaming from it by a guilt-infested nightmare? She shivered from the cold trapped inside herself.

7

Falling rain formed a white-yellow cloud along the length of Rye Thornton's motorcycle headlight beam. He felt it on his face and arms, felt it vibrate into the chest and shoulders of his leather jacket. Usually he loved the rain, relished the terrible fury locked in those dark clouds, hung on every lightning-fast threat of it. He used to sit on the front porch expectantly, just watching the swirling clouds with ...

His memory faded abruptly, darting away on quick-turning falcon's wings. Leaving him empty and cold despite the warm rain.

He fumbled for the name mentally but couldn't find it. Why? Why wasn't it there? The memory had seemed like such a gentle thing and had fallen into his consciousness so easily. Not like the nightmares that gave him headaches and woke him in the darkness with the feel of cold and clammy sweat all over his body.

He tilted his head up for a moment, closing his eyes as he opened his mouth and caught some of the falling rain on his tongue. The Harley rumbled between his legs, handling roughly now that they were on the dirt roads leading up to the pickup site.

A horn sounded a brief warning to his left. Two beeps a quarter-beat apart.

He looked back and swerved to miss the armadillo that had stopped in the middle of the muddy road. Its two fire-bright eyes flashed redly at him as he passed it, and he saw its blurred outlines scuttle toward the trees as the rider behind him topped the rise.

He did a quick head-count as the ragged line of Death's Enforcers spread out ahead and behind him. Nine men. The empty space left by Rattle was obvious to him even in the dark and filled with a silence that sucked away the ear-splitting grumble of the sleds.

Rattle.

Lot of memories with that guy. Not good memories, but ones he could still reach out and touch. Which, with the way his mind had been working lately, was something. Losing even a scab like Rattle left a void in his world now, and that didn't say a lot for the condition of his world.

Rattle's death wasn't just a lost path down memory lane. It also symbolized that an assault had been struck against his command, endangering his mission.

Thornton geared down to make an upcoming turn, flicking the shift lever and squeezing the clutch as though he'd been doing it every day of his life. He recoiled from the sudden thought. He had been doing it every day of his adult life, hadn't he? Before the Death's Enforcers there had been other gangs. Hell, he'd ridden with the Angels in L.A., went down some roads on his own. Him and a scooter. It had been that way as long as he could remember it, he reassured himself. Still, he wished the uncertainty would fade and that he could be more afraid of the cops who were sure to be looking for them instead of being afraid of what was locked inside his own head.

For a moment he wished the cops could catch them. Then it would be all over.

Wouldn't it?

The headache was beginning again, forming a throbbing spike that ran through his temples.

That was crazy thinking! He'd been inside before. Didn't need no more of that shit. Yeah, and it had been a hell of a long three months in... Where the hell had he been to prison? It didn't matter. Wherever. It had seemed like an eternity. Hadn't it?

He shifted uncomfortably on the seat, knowing the unevenness of the dirt road was going to play hell with the headache. It was bad enough without the jarring and bumping. Harleys were made to fly, baby; the streets were the only sky they knew. His arms felt leaden from hanging on to the bars. The black leather gloves felt like another layer of skin soaking into the flesh.

What the hell had gone wrong at the marina? Rattle wasn't supposed to end up dead like that. Not even a scumbag like Rattle, who had a thing for fourteen-year-old chicks and hearing them scream. They were supposed to be protected.

Somebody had promised him that. That much he knew, even if he couldn't remember who it was.

The front tire skidded into a muddy rut, splashing out the rainwater as it twisted like a dying snake.

Thornton willed himself to become a part of the bike, becoming a live nerve wired to the big-hearted Harley, controlling it and seducing it at the same time. The scooter kept its head and didn't go down, the rear tire spinning threateningly before finding traction.

Once he had the direction leveled out again, he slipped a hand under the leather jacket to make sure the S&W 645 hadn't been lost along the way. There. Still in the shoulder leather. Feeling better, he gave himself over to the road and chased away the memories, confident they wouldn't be entirely lost. They came to haunt him whenever they chose, anyway.

The choice of words sent a shiver down his spine that was connected somehow to things he couldn't remember. He dodged the questions, knowing they would suck him inside himself again if he gave even one the chance.

Two hours east of Miami, using care to check for potential police roadblocks along the way, had found them at their current location on the fringes of the Everglades swampland. The way out had been his idea. Not Corsini's. He hadn't told the man that, hadn't told his band of men until they were fleeing the marina area. Only he and the pilot of the plane they were to meet knew about this rendezvous.

Thornton had learned a long time ago to never open himself up to complete inspection of his ways and plans by a potential enemy. And the younger Corsini definitely filled the bill in that respect. Vincent Corsini was skewed one hundred eighty degrees from his father. Sal was from the old school, knowing a proper way to do everything, demanding respect. Vincent, and you didn't call the guy Vince or Vinnie for damn sure, went after money in the quickest way possible, and if it wasn't proper, then tough shit. Respect was something he didn't care about, either. Because Vincent Corsini had learned fear was a much stronger motivator.

Where Sal had been a practitioner of form, his son found new schemes every day, and that was how Thornton had linked up with Vincent Corsini, shepherding ten million dollars' worth of cocaine back to Toronto for a down payment on one of Vincent's bigger deals behind his father's back. Of course, Vincent hadn't told Thornton even that much, but from being around the younger Corsini during the past six months, he'd learned some of the man's patterns.

A war of behind-the-scenes attrition was taking place in Toronto. And the son was ruthlessly planning to remove his father's power, piece by bloody piece, while the elder Corsini was restricted by form. Until his son made an overt threat toward him, Sal refused to take any real action. In the meantime Vincent was establishing himself as the new man to deal with.

Thornton pulled his scooter over and flagged down his lieutenant on the Miami run.

Skeeter Davis was a shaggy brute of a man, long and wolf lean astride the flathead. He put both booted feet down and walked himself on the bike forward as he came to a stop beside Thornton.

"Check it out, Spider," Skeeter said as they watched the stream of bikers pass by in single file. His beard split in a grin, and light reflected from his crooked teeth and the skull-and-crossbones earring mounted on his headband. "Two hours later, and we're still haulin' ass. We deserve a fuckin' bonus for pullin' this off for your Mafia pal."

"The bonus is going to be getting out of here alive, Skeeter."

Skeeter shook his head and laughed. "Don't get to be a downer, man. So they took Rattle out. Not that big of a loss, if you know what I mean? I mean, old Rattle, he was good for parties and bullshit, but he didn't exactly have it crankin' upstairs."

Thornton nodded. "Just the same, Skeeter, I want you to post Crazy Ron and Brokedick behind us at the next checkpoint. Have them stay there until they see the plane coming down."

"Brokedick ain't gonna like that, leader man. He's gonna figure you for tryin' to leave him behind."

"Tough shit, Skeeter. Tell the son of a bitch he'll do what I tell him to, or I'll bury him in this fuckin' swamp. You make sure he understands that."

"Okay, okay, I read you, guy. I'll make sure he stays myself."

"Hell, he may be the lucky one. Him and Crazy Ron both. If things get hairy and the dope fuzz is on top of the situation that we might have skipped in this direction instead of north, at least they'll have a running head start.''

"One thing I wouldn't want to be a party to tonight," Skeeter said, "is a fuckin' swamp scramble in all this dark.''

"It might come to that.''

"Maybe. But I doubt it. You see, my man, I been keepin' an eye on you ever since you started running the club. I mean, you're no great shakes when it comes to cuttin' loose and lettin' your hair down, but you got this 'in' with Corsini and it's let us cut some pretty good deals for ourselves. Take this dope scam, for instance. We're making the buy using his money, bought us a fuckin' bunch of nose candy with it, then we're out here in the middle of nowheresville with a plane you set up for. I been thinkin' it'd be just as easy for us to aim that plane somewheres else besides Toronto at this point and live high on the hog for a while.''

Making his voice cold, Thornton said, "You got any more thoughts like that in your system, Skeeter, you'd better leave them behind here. Talk like that will get you killed when we get back to Toronto.''

Skeeter grinned. "It's just talk, Spider. Just talk. Chill it out, man. I don't know what's got you walkin' around all soft footed on this deal. We're puttin' it together. Just the way you said we would. We lost Rattle. It was a bad break. Coulda happened to anybody. But we're free and flying clear of this whole scene in just a few minutes. You got guts, Spider, and a whole shit-pot full of luck since I known you. I'd hate to see you pussy out now.''

"You won't," Thornton promised as he dropped the shift lever into first and eased out the clutch. "Get Crazy Ron and Brokedick and do like I told you.''

Skeeter gave him a mock salute and another grin.

Thornton put it behind him, wishing the sick feeling would leave his stomach, knowing that was sometimes the way it was and you had to trust those gut feelings in this kind of job.

Job.

The word ran cold water down his spine, and he tried to track down the cause for the feeling. It eluded him, leaving a scum-slick trail through his thoughts.

He twisted the throttle, accelerating dangerously across the potholed dirt road, aware that the Harley could be torn from under him at any time but not caring and not knowing why.

"THERE'S THE PLANE!" Moon yelled.

Thornton grimaced, looking in the direction the biker was pointing. "Pipe down," he ordered as he stepped forward and lifted his binoculars to his eyes. "For all you wild-asses know, that's a winged narc up there and his buddies are cruising the bushes for us now. Last thing we need to give them is a fuckin' sonar of our position."

The biker grumbled, then kept quiet.

Tracking the plane, Thornton saw that it was an amphibious Cessna of the same model he'd set up through his connection in Toronto. He felt better. At least the plans were okay even if the head wasn't.

The bikers shifted uneasily around him as the plane skidded on its pontoons in the small lagoon in front of them. Something irritated him from the back of his mind but he ignored it, figuring it was more of the strange memories that coiled inside his head.

Coming to a stop, the plane floated loosely on top of the swamp. The pilot stepped out on a pontoon and threw out an anchor.

Looking over the motley crew of eight men behind him, each with a bundle of cocaine strapped across his back, Thornton said, "Okay, let's move it. Keep it close and keep it simple. We aren't out of the woods yet."

"That's for fuckin' sure," someone grumbled.

"I still don't like the idea of leaving my scooter here," another one said. "Me and that hog been down some trails."

Thornton said, "You don't like it so much, Moose, then give me that pack and ride it back to Toronto." He held out a hand, waiting.

The big man grinned. "No fuckin' way, Spider. With the money we make off this gig, I'll buy me another."

"And love her just as much," Crazy Ron said.

The bikers all laughed.

Thornton shook his head at the craziness they displayed, wondering how the bikers could seem like misguided children at one minute and murderous brutes the next. Just as he'd been told. He wished he could remember who had told him that. But he'd known that anyway, hadn't he?

Thornton led the way into the swamp water, trying to keep his mind off what might be gliding through its depths only inches from his legs. It felt cold, and it seemed like the mud on the bottom was ninety percent glue.

Someone yelped, then cursed and asked for help because they'd lost a boot in the mud. Everybody laughed but nobody volunteered, and even the bootless biker didn't give it a second thought.

The itchy sensation at the base of Thornton's brain spread down his shoulders. He kept checking the banks of the swamp, waiting expectantly for police vehicles to explode into view at any time.

The water was up to his waist by the time he reached the plane. Cursing their slowness, the pilot extended a hand to help him up on the pontoon.

A buzzsaw kicked loose in Thornton's ear, muffling startled screams of astonishment as surely as the black swamp water below them would.

Ragged holes appeared across the pilot's legs, spilling the man into the murky depths under his plane.

Even as he threw himself sideways, Thornton was aware of a line of bullets chasing across the surface of the Cessna, chewing the metal to reach him. Something ripped across his upper chest, bringing a stinging pain that flooded his whole right side. Then he was slammed violently in the chest and felt his breath go out of him in a long cough. His head hit the plane, but it was only an incidental pain. Nothing compared to the tremendous impact that had knocked the wind out of his lungs.

He felt the swamp water close greasy fingers over his face.

His vision was stained by flotsam in the water, leaving dark specks scattered across the surface, illuminated by the running lights of the plane.

Water filled his ears, and he couldn't find his balance. Fingers trailed through the oozing mud as he realized he wasn't dying after all.

His lungs aching from the strain of holding his breath, he swam below the surface of the swamp. Back toward the shore. To safety.

Vibrations, carried by the water, touched him, made him aware someone was moving nearby.

A body touched him as he surfaced. The feel of wet hair caressed his cheek as the odor of gasoline and motor oil flooded his nostrils with a dozen other scents he couldn't identify. The air tasted cool. It hurt to breathe.

He stayed by the corpse, unable to keep from looking at the ruined face and recognizing it as Brokedick. He shivered, scanning back toward the Cessna, getting his bearings. He wondered how badly he was injured.

Two figures scrambled up the side of the plane. One was Skeeter, holding a mini-Uzi Thornton hadn't even known the man had. The other was a biker named Hooter, who had always been one of Skeeter's main hangers-on.

Thornton reached for his Smith, discovering that at least one of the bullets had hit it instead of him. He slid the .45 free, barely keeping his face out of the water, resisting the urge to spit when the brackish water slipped into his mouth.

"Get the rest of the coke," Skeeter ordered as he threw two packs into the interior of the plane. The pontoons rocked with the motion of the big man's movements, bobbing up and down in the water as the craft slowly eddied in a radius the length of the anchor line.

Slitting his eyes against the pain and the sudden glare of the flashlight Hooter shone across the surface of the swamp, Thornton pulled the hammer of the .45 back under the water. He thought it was soundless, but he couldn't be sure because the bass thumping in his head took away most of the exterior sounds.

Hooter cursed and tramped through the water, the flashlight's beam a jerky counterbalance to his movements. "Are you sure they're all dead?" the burly man asked.

A knife gleamed in Skeeter's fist as he cut the straps holding another parcel of the cocaine.

Thornton watched the body slide back under the dark water after Skeeter kicked it away. No more Moon. Roll call was getting shorter all the time. Only now it was being eaten away from the inside. Like a cancer. He locked his fingers around the butt of the Smith, wishing he still had all of the feeling in his extremities, hoping he was still gripping the pistol tightly enough. He continued to bring his arm up slowly, biting back the pain that ripped through his chest. He prayed that the .45 hadn't been damaged by the bullet that had caromed off it.

"If they aren't dead, Hooter, finish the job. I think I hear the pilot floppin' around on the other side of the plane, and I'll take care of him. Don't take any chances with any of this crew. Spider lined up a bunch of hardcases for this run. You can bet'cher ass if we leave any of them alive, they'll start lookin' for us as soon as they can walk."

Thornton gulped more air, willing himself to wait. *They'd turn on you, Ryan—don't ever forget that.* The words drifted through his mind like reefer fog, twisting and turning through a reality of their own. He tired to look behind the fog, tried to find the face of the voice that had told him that. An outline took shape. Then he felt his hand brush across someone else's in the darkness of the memory, felt his lips meet someone else's, his lungs dragged in someone else's ragged breath.

He recoiled, barely able to restrain a cry of pain, releasing a mewling sound that was covered over by a blast of autofire.

He blinked his eyes, fighting clear of the memory.

Hooter looked down at the corpse he'd riddled, and Thornton could see distaste on the big man's face.

"What the hell happened?" Skeeter demanded from the plane.

"Thought old Crazy Ron was still alive," Hooter said sheepishly. "Guess he wasn't after all, but I wanted to make sure."

"Did you shoot into that coke?"

"No, man, I took his face off. Damn flashlight made his eyes look like they was lookin' back at me. The coke's okay." He held up the pack to prove his point.

"Just be careful of the coke, man. You damage it in this water, and you can kiss it goodbye."

"I know, man. Stay off my back." Hooter threw the pack toward the plane, and it fell a couple yards short.

"Get them closer, damn it. Do you think I like wadin' through this shit?"

Hooter whirled around angrily. "You want to wade out here awhile, Skeeter? Turn over a few of these bodies yourself? These fuckin' Uzis make a hell of a mess when you turn them loose the way we did."

"No, I 'pologize, man. I'm just ready to get the show on the road."

"Me an' you both, brother," Hooter grumbled. "Me an' you both."

Thornton waited till Skeeter was in the water, reaching for the floating pack, to make his move, knowing the biker would be unable to react as quickly in the swamp as he would have on the plane.

Locking his boots into the mud, he stood straight up out of the water, ignoring the pain that flared through his side. He dropped the .45 into the center of Hooter's broad chest less than fifteen feet away and squeezed the trigger in rapid fire. He shot the man four times, swiveling in the water as the body fell, tracking back toward Skeeter.

The biker was a dim shadow skating across the top of the swamp, flailing for the Uzi slung from his neck.

Thornton punched three 185-grain hollowpoints at the man, shoving aside the dead body of Brokedick as he pushed himself forward through the mud. An angry scream filled his ears as he charged and it took him a second to realize the sound was coming from his own throat.

Skeeter went down before the onslaught.

A splashing noise grabbed his attention.

Thornton turned, leveling the Smith.

Hooter's head broke the surface weakly and the man bellowed in unrestrained fury.

Two more bullets from the .45 kicked the big man's skull backward, and the rest of his body followed. The slide kicked blew back as the magazine emptied.

His breath was rasping in his lungs, and pain constricted his chest, but Thornton slammed a fresh magazine home and made his way to Skeeter's position. He reached for the man's coat to haul him closer, then stabbed the heated muzzle of the pistol through the swamp water against the biker's face.

"Easy, Skeeter. Move easy or I swear I'll take the top of your head off." He pulled the man free of the water.

Skeeter choked, spluttering water weakly. Blood slipped across his pallid lips with it, but he smiled cockily. "Well, well, my man, it looks like you done kilt me." He coughed up more blood, darker than the swamp water it floated on.

"You're not dead yet, Skeeter."

"As good as, Spider. I can't feel my legs and I can tell I'm all tore up inside. Bleedin' in there, man. I can feel it."

Holding the man's face only inches from his own, struggling against the mixture of emotions racing inside his head, Thornton said, "Why, Skeeter? Was it the money?"

The eyelids fluttered closed for a moment, then flickered back open. "I won't shit you, man. I'm dying. Got nothin' to win by holdin' back on you now." He coughed, more weakly than before. "Cut a deal behind your back, Spider. Thought I had me a winnin' hand. Didn't know you'd be so fuckin' hard to kill."

"What kind of deal?"

"Young Vinnie, my man. He wanted you put down. Said if I delivered the coke instead of you, I'd get the money he was supposed to pay you." The words halted, as a paroxysm of coughing shook his body and choked him off. "I took the deal, Spider, only 'cause I couldn't turn it down. Never had somethin' so sweet shoved in my face before. I'd been thinkin' about me and Hooter trying' to heist it anyway and cut a deal with somebody else, never show Canada our faces again. Vinnie's lined up those out-of-town buyers. Figured me an' ol' Hooter coulda done the same, with a little luck." Spittle slipped through his lips, and he gave Thornton a wink and a bloody grin. "Thing ol' Vinnie didn't figure on is me gettin' kilt. Or maybe he ciphered that in somewhere and just figured on cuttin' down the odds stacked against him goin' in. Maybe by livin' long enough to tell you the true of it, I'm still gonna be part of the team. You get the chance, tell him I sent you. Best regards.''

Thornton used both hands to hold the dying man, feeling hot tears burn at the back of his eyes. Skeeter had been a part of his life for so long. They'd been friends. Even though the man had tried to kill him, they'd been friends. Knowing the biker mentality as he did, he knew that for Skeeter killing him hadn't been personal. It had only been one colossal joke, one that Thornton should have been able to understand even if he didn't empathize with it. *Knowing the biker mentality?* The thought seemed disjointed, incongruous with his feelings. A sensation of outsideness while inside the situation. They'll turn on you the first chance they get, the unidentified memory warned him again.

Skeeter shivered in his arms, and a rattling sounded in the man's throat.

"Goddamn you, Skeeter," Thornton swore as memories of the past few months trickled in and out of his thoughts. "Goddamn you for getting killed."

"Had to be one of us, bro', had to be one of us." Skeeter lifted his head off Thornton's chest and smiled, the lights dimming in his eyes. "Been one hell of a ride, though."

Thornton watched the biker's head slump forward, striking the injured area of his chest painfully. He held the man for a time, trying to find some sense of himself as he felt the swamp muck curling around his feet. Damn it. He'd never felt so lost and alone. Or had he? Other memories crowded in at him, unable to break through whatever barrier was keeping them out. He reached for them, feeling the slackness of Skeeter's body against his own, feeling the chill of the emptiness that threatened to consume him from inside. A tendril poked through the barrier in his mind, extending a name that led to other memories. Thad. God, he'd never had the chance to hold Thad like this. He recoiled from the memory in sheer terror, almost losing his balance in the swamp because the image that threatened to spill loose was so intensely physical.

He blinked back tears, wishing he had the strength to pursue those thoughts that beckoned to him so seductively from the curtains of his mind, knowing subconsciously that if they were allowed into the reality of this moment, they would suck him dry. And an emotionless husk couldn't do what he intended to do. Couldn't take the fire of vengeance to Vinnie Corsini's front door and burn his house down.

Thornton intended to. No matter what it cost him.

He turned his mind from the past to the present and released Skeeter's body, wishing he had a better place to leave the man than in the fetid swamp water where anything might feed on him. Skeeter disappeared under the murky water.

"Spider?" a voice called, and Thornton looked toward the sound of the man's voice, the .45 extended before him.

"Hey, man, it's me. Wings."

The silhouette hanging on the bobbing wing of the Cessna fell into quick target acquisition. Thornton squinted through the shadows, making out the Baltimore Orioles jacket the pilot wore. "Are you okay?"

"Shot up some," the pilot said as he struggled to get around the plane, "but still hanging in there. Couple bullets went through my legs. Had worse in Nam. I'd've helped you put those two away, Spider, but I didn't have no piece. Wasn't expectin' any trouble since this was your score. Until tonight you've always had the velvet touch on stuff we put together."

Thornton released the hammer on the Smith and stepped toward the Cessna, feeling Skeeter's submerged form brush against his leg for a second before the body drifted away. "Can you fly?"

A pained grin split the pilot's pallid face. "Do I got a choice, hot shot?"

"No," Thornton replied honestly. "Anyone could have heard what happened tonight. Or seen something."

"All the more reason to get our asses up in the air."

Thornton nodded and clambered aboard the Cessna after the wounded pilot. He pulled the door closed behind him, looking out over the swamp and the dead memories as the engines shuddered to life.

He pressed a hand against the window, seeking out something but not knowing what. Feeling nothing but the void.

The Death's Enforcers hadn't been much, an errant thought told him, but he had the impression they'd been all he had left.

The Cessna slowly turned on the surface of the swamp. "Where to?" the pilot asked.

"Toronto."

Wings's face turned sour as he checked the instruments. "Corsini'll know somethin' went wrong down here, Spider. You can bet'cher ass on that."

Thornton nodded. "Got nowhere else to go. We've got a plane full of hot product and no place else to off-load it easily. We know there are people in Toronto looking for a quick deal. We can try to link up with them."

"Corsini's not gonna let that slide, ace. He set up this deal."

"Then turned around and fucked it up," Thornton added. The swamp faded into black film devoid of details as the plane skipped forward, pulled by the twin engines. "And one way or another, I'm going to get Vinnie Corsini off my ass once and forever."

"Vinnie's gonna be lookin' for you if you try that, Spider."

"I know."

"You're gonna be icing on the cake for ol' Vinnie if what Skeeter said was true. You slip up, and he'll get you and the coke."

"If I slip." Thornton looked at the pilot as the plane shrugged free of gravity and banked tight. "And anyway, I'm poison. Ask any of those boys down there. I linked the Enforcers to the Corsini Family through Vinnie, helped set up this deal, then led them here to die."

"It was a sweet deal, Spider. Ain't nobody gonna blame you for tryin'. Coulda made a lot of people a lot of money if people hadn't got so greedy."

"Yeah, well, I'm going to make sure Vinnie chokes on this deal, too," Thornton promised, focusing on the rage locked inside him.

8

Mobile news units jammed the street, vying for parking space with police cruisers and regular traffic in front of the police station.

Mack Bolan drifted through the pedestrian flow, clad in a brown bomber jacket, jeans, cowboy boots and a Western shirt of muted earth tones. The cowboy hat he wore served to soften his features with shadows. Not typical wear for a balmy Miami night, but the ensemble attracted enough attention to satisfy onlookers that they easily had him pegged as a tourist type. The silenced Beretta rode in shoulder leather, and a Ka-bar was sheathed inside one of the boots.

He gazed at the entrance to the precinct, noting the staggered groups of people going and coming. According to the police scanner he had been listening to in his rental car, he was sure the DEA people were still at the precinct.

He wished he could have brought a cup of coffee along but knew that if he had, the policemen he would be seeing in the building would demand his press pass, too. The reporters stayed up late and got up early, working to fit the pieces together on their latest story. He didn't have press ID, but he did have a simple black briefcase, containing photocopies of the information he'd received from Hunsaker, which would buy him at least temporary credibility. The originals were in a Greyhound bus locker not far from the marina. If he failed to interest Silverman in the deal he'd worked up, he intended to drop the copies anyway and let Brognola send a Justice agent to pick up the originals to make sure the information was acted on.

A female reporter slammed a hand against the metal rail separating the up and down side of the steps as she brushed by Bolan. "Goddamn tinhorn desk sergeant," she swore. "He's not gonna get away with this shit as easily as he thinks, Byron."

Bolan paused, letting the skinny cameraman follow her.

The cameraman mouthed a silent thank-you to Bolan as he passed. His glasses had slid to the end of his nose, and his shoulder looked as though the Camcorder was rapidly becoming too heavy for him. "Take it easy, Carrie," the cameraman said in a soothing voice.

"Screw taking it easy, Byron. The press has a right to know what's going on. Fuckin' First Amendment we're talkin' about here. We got dead bodies scattered all over that marina, and Dick Tracy up there has got his thumb up his ass."

"He said the detective in charge would be issuing a statement to the press within the hour."

Bolan watched the reporter whirl suddenly and place a pointed finger against the cameraman's thin chest. Her face was taut with anger.

"Goddamn it, Byron! I make the press releases for our station, you got that? Me! Not some cretin with a swivel chair pinned to his ass. Now get that camera set up so we can roll. When these guys get around to releasing anything pertinent, this will all be old news. I want to get some footage in front of this precinct, then we'll go see if we can scare up one of those dead bodies. If we can't, I want a sheet with ketchup stains and somebody who wants to earn a quick twenty dollars. You got that?"

By the time Bolan reached the glass doors leading inside the police station, the reporter had dropped her hostility and was projecting sincerity and sugary sweetness. Her voice had brightened considerably as she launched into a tirade against local drug czars and highlighted the heroic efforts of police detectives to clean up the Miami Beach area.

The air inside the station house felt cool and crisp, heavy with expectation.

Bolan moved into the press of bodies in the lounge area off to one side of the desk sergeant. He waited till a stringer for a local radio station filed his story, including statements read from a small spiral-bound notebook complete with quote-unquotes, then took the phone because it allowed visual access to the main hallway.

Voices of the men and women grumbling about the lack of sleep and the lack of police cooperation on the story provided a background that seemed as if it had been culled from another world. He tapped in Brognola's home number, then gave the operator a credit card calling number that traced back to the Justice Department under a safe alias.

"Yeah?" Brognola sounded more awake this time.

"Hello, Hal," Bolan responded as he stood to one side of the pay phone so he could scan everyone coming and going through the foyer. "Have you had any luck at that end?"

"Some. But it's still too early to turn up more than the bare bones on the stuff you wanted. My advice is to get your ass out of the area until Aaron and I can get you armed with more Intel and some kind of cover."

Bolan grinned to himself as he looked out over the assembled cops and reporters. "I'll take it into consideration, guy, but for right now I've got to go with my instincts, and they say whatever is going to break on this thing will break before morning."

A group of reporters and cameramen who'd been conversing in the corner suddenly broke out in gales of laughter.

"Where are you, Striker?"

"At a pay phone in a police station, about thirty feet from the sergeant on duty, where the DEA team has camped to oversee their operation."

Brognola was silent for a moment, then Bolan heard him crunching on antacid tablets. "I hope you know what you're doing, Striker, because I've heard that area is already heated up. And there's an APB out on a big guy dressed all in black who raided a biker bar, put in an appearance at a marina where he shot a drug smuggler who was the focus of a local vice raid and stole an unmarked vehicle from the crime scene."

"Like I said, Hal, it's been a busy night. This thing is breaking pretty fast. The problem is, I haven't quite put my finger on what it is that's going down."

"I'm not going to be able to demystify you all at once, but I may be able to shed some light on your present situation."

Bolan shifted, making his face take on a bored expression for the benefit of the handful of people who glanced at him curiously. He cast a few wistful glances at his watch as though he had better things to do than listen to the person on the other end of the connection. Most news people were good observers with a memory for details, and he wanted to make them remember an impression he created specifically for them. A big guy who was obviously in a hurry to get out of the scene. Not someone who was taking an interest in anything going on around him.

"Frank Judson is the supervisor over the operation the DEA is working at your end of things. I couldn't get any poop on exactly what or who the subject is, but my contact at the FBI told me Judson's been involved in this case over six or eight months. And it was important enough to take precedence over what is happening down there."

"What is his usual beat, Hal? The Death's Enforcers bikers are from Toronto, and his partner seemed inordinately interested in them rather than the product connections at this end.''

"New York and points north. I got a glimmer of an impression that the ultimate prize Judson and his group are going for is home-based in Toronto."

"Meaning the Corsini Family?"

"Meaning maybe. Like I said, whatever file Judson is currently working on is something out of reach for my guy at the Bureau. But it seems to add up that way, doesn't it?"

"Yeah." Bolan watched the desk sergeant take a call and scribble on a pad. Several of the reporters in the lounge area stopped their conversations for a moment as interest perked up. "What kind of guy is he?"

"From what I've been able to kick over so far, Judson has a good name in the DEA. A real hard-line kind of agent who doesn't mind putting in the hours and expects his crew to do the same. He goes by the book as long as it suits him, but doesn't mind bending the rules as long as it doesn't interfere with his conviction rate. He's got a rep for putting together airtight cases from his younger years with the DEA."

"And now?"

"Now things are getting tougher for him. Everybody's going semilegit these days, Striker. It's getting harder to separate criminal dealings from honest business. The guys laundering money are taking more time and more care with their handiwork. Hell, play your cards right, and you can finance a damn good business for yourself then leave the scut work to guys still hungry for a dollar. You've seen this game in action before."

"Only then everybody was wanting to get rich overnight."

"Yeah."

"So, we're only guessing our guy is interested in the Corsinis?"

"Judson's been at the head of other probes into the Corsini Family. If the DEA is mounting another tilt at the Corsini windmill, Judson would be the logical choice."

"Even though he hasn't pinned anything on them before?"

"He hasn't succeeded in getting any dirt on the Corsini Family personally, Striker, but that doesn't mean he hasn't put together some effective operations against them. Usually his undercover operations stop somewhere in what is assumed to be middle management for the Corsinis. He's cost them some along the way, and they know it."

"What could interest the Corsini Family in cocaine from Miami?" Bolan asked.

"That I don't know."

Bolan let it spin around in his head, dealing cards out for the players who were sure to be involved. Judson and his DEA team on one side. The Corsini Family on another. The Miami connection scanned as background for the events so far, but it was yet to be seen where the final action would take place. Maybe Toronto, and the Death's Enforcers acted as the bridge between...yeah, but how many places did that bridge extend? Also, the biker gang had to evacuate the area with an APB out on them. If Judson did have a guy undercover in the ranks of the bikers, the federal agent must have been able to ensure them safe passage báck to Toronto. Then there was the uncertainty about how many of the local cops were willing to let the bust slide by.

"How do the bikers connect up with the Corsini Family?" Bolan asked.

The conversations around him had picked up again, sounding like a dull roar.

"Through Vincent Corsini," Brognola replied. "Salvatore Corsini, the old man of the family, has been strictly small-time his entire career. Kept his finger in small pies in the Toronto area—gambling, girls, clubs and passed out a few contract executions over the years. He started to blossom a bit after the Commisso Family went belly-up to an investigation by the Mounties, but he still doesn't deal in drugs.''

"Then where's the connection, Hal?"

"My Bureau buddy suggested Vincent, the son. Sal Corsini has held true to one maxim his whole adult life—live big but be small potatoes. Apparently Vincent doesn't want to live his life in the shadow of his father. Another source, questioned discreetly without being told about the Miami involvement, tied Vincent Corsini to the Death's Enforcers. According to the lady DA I talked to in Fredericton, Corsini the younger is suspected of working deals through the bikers. Contracting hits, extortion and intimidation and maybe drugs.''

"But it's not solid?"

"If it was, the Toronto people would have closed house on Vincent Corsini before now. People who know things about Vincent Corsini's illegal business interests have turned up dead and missing when it came time to make a statement. From what the lady told me, Corsini is an animal. Nothing like his father, who still comports himself like an old-world gentleman.''

"Read, Mafia."

"Exactly, Striker. Vincent Corsini is dangerous. A volatile man who's rumored to handle most of his own hatchet work and to enjoy it.''

"And Judson may have placed his man in the middle of this with nowhere to go.''

"Maybe." Brognola sighed. "Damn it, Striker, I read it the same way you do. Judson's just the type to try putting a guy in that deep, too. He's approaching mandatory retirement. This investigation could be his last chance at the brass ring as a DEA agent. He's the kind of guy who'd want to go out with a book contract, a movie deal and a hit album waiting in his near future."

"And whatever happened to the undercover guy would be just a tough break."

"Yeah."

"Hell of a guy the agency has working for them."

"Not everybody is like that."

"I know, Hal. I'm just tired, that's all." But that wasn't all, and Bolan didn't try fooling himself. He knew what it was like to be on the run, unable to trust anyone, living each movement and every moment in the fear that somehow it might reveal who he was. Even the arm's-length life-style he had agreed to with the Justice Department had placed him only a heartbeat away from the fugitive range. Judson had been on whatever operation he was supervising for six to eight months. Perhaps longer. Bolan felt confident in assuming the undercover man had been deep at least that long. Six to eight months. God, he could still remember what it had been like during the early days of his war against the Mafia, constantly on the run with no friendly hand in sight and no safe harbor to retreat to. But he had been accustomed to that. He'd exchanged a thick green jungle for a concrete one, exchanged fighting an outside battle against the laws of nature for one against the laws of man. You couldn't stay civilized in the jungle. Not if you were to survive. And you didn't remain unmarked by that jungle, either. How was Judson's operative scarred by his stay in the jungle he'd been thrown into?

Survival was something Mack Bolan had been good at for a long time. Those traits had been born in war in Vietnam and brought to maturity under the withering fire of criminals and terrorists around the globe. Somewhere in there, he knew, those wars had become the driving force of the man.

It wasn't that way for the guy Judson had ordered down into the trenches of the Death's Enforcers.

That guy still had a lot to lose.

With the deaths of his family, Sergeant Mack Bolan had enlisted in a war to save humanity from the criminals. He'd been around long enough to know it would be a long engagement. And he was drawn to it like a moth to a flame because it gave a sense to his losses. Because he could do it and couldn't step away from the duty he found there.

Judson's man was good. Otherwise he wouldn't have lasted as long as he apparently had. But how much longer would the man be able to survive the high-stakes game he found himself in?

"Striker?"

"Yeah, Hal."

"Are you okay?"

"Yeah, just involved in sorting this thing out."

Brognola was quiet for a moment. "You're not coming out of this, are you?"

"Not yet."

"I wish you'd reconsider that."

"I have. Something doesn't scan right here. There's a lot of pressure on this operation. I can feel it. This thing isn't just going to break, Hal. It's going to come apart at the seams. A lot of good people could get hurt when it does."

"I know."

"What have you got for me on the guy's partner?"

"Piper Silverman is a stand-up lady and a decent operative. She's been with the DEA for the last four years. She was a uniform for the NYPD before that. College degree. My contact also let me know this operation is her first shot at being involved with an undercover in a supervisory capacity."

"She's overseeing an undercover?"

"Yeah."

"Did you get a name?"

"No. You can only press a casual friendship so far without inciting suspicion. The DEA are a cagey bunch and tend to have long memories. They have to for the kind of work they do."

Translated, that meant Brognola couldn't afford to be dragged into the situation if things in Miami overheated and blew up in the Executioner's face. Bolan knew the head Fed was uncomfortable with having to even come that close to defining the almost one-way relationship the government had with the Executioner. To Bolan, though, it was business as usual.

Bolan said, "I understand, Hal."

"I was afraid you would. Damn it, Mack, you know I hate drawing lines around anything you involve yourself in, but we don't even know if this one will pay off for anyone. Too many people are already involved. I don't want to see you get burned."

Bolan smiled grimly, putting warmth in his voice. "I don't, either."

"Give me some time," Brognola said. "I've got Aaron getting a package together for one Michael Belasko, who works for the Justice Department. We can stonewall questions long enough to get you in and out, provide a background that will stand up to a surface scrutiny."

Bolan watched the desk sergeant rub his eyes tiredly, saw the man track across the room again and focus on the briefcase in his hand for a moment. He knew he'd been on the phone too long. Even a handful of the reporters were starting to feel their jaded curiosity kick to life; the full frontal stares were shifting to surreptitious glances. "I don't think the situation has the time to give."

Brognola fell silent.

Bolan knew the man was filled with bleak thoughts of his own but didn't let them touch him. The Executioner lived on the edge of life, and the Fed knew that. Brognola had the mission to look at, the planning, the objectives. Bolan focused on the numbers and kicked his plays into operation between heartbeats.

"If there's anything I can do, Striker..."

"Can you get me a plane on standby? I have the feeling this thing is going to go international before it runs its course."

"That I can do. I'll set up a private charter in the Belasko name, since the Bear is already plugging that into the computers."

"Chances are, I'll need clearance to land in Toronto, too."

"I'll take care of it."

"Thanks, Hal."

"Stay in touch, big guy."

Bolan said he would, then broke the connection and drifted back through the glass door to the balmy world under the fast-approaching dawn.

ALMOST TWENTY MINUTES LATER, Bolan saw Piper Silverman leaving the police station. Most of the news teams had vacated the street, leaving only a few die-hard newspaper reporters and people not directly involved with the electronic media. Bolan had learned most of that from monitoring the conversations of the men and women who'd visited the small café across the street from the police station.

When he saw the DEA agent walk down the steps, he took his cowboy hat from the booth he'd occupied since leaving the police station, slipped it on his head and trailed behind the woman on the opposite side of the street.

Carrying the briefcase made him feel awkward and exposed as he walked down the sidewalk, one among the day's early risers. The coffee he'd had while at the diner helped him stay awake but also made him feel hollowed out and drained. He needed rest but couldn't stop pushing himself until he found out where the trail he was pursuing led.

The whole situation was a mass of loose ends and had a pervasive sensation of falseness. Maybe if the local vice cops had made a bigger score at the marina, it wouldn't have been so glaringly obvious to him.

He moved loosely and easily, distancing the woman's long stride so that he continued to trail slightly behind her. He regretted the selection of cowboy boots as he moved in her wake. The soles spanged against the wet concrete, and he was sure if Silverman hadn't had her mind occupied elsewhere, she would have heard him.

He crossed the street when he saw her reach into her purse and come to a halt beside a late-model Ford sedan with rental plates. A cab whizzed by him, the horn raucously honking the driver's frustration with the narrow miss. He felt water splash across the back of his jeans.

Silverman looked up as the horn sounded, noting his straightforward approach at once.

He saw the puzzlement on her face. Then recognition sparked in her eyes. She reached under her raincoat.

Before she could bring her gun into view, Bolan had the 93-R in his hand and said, "Leave it there."

Her hand froze, but he could see in her dark eyes that her first impulse was to go for the weapon.

He closed the distance and held his hand out. "Put it in the briefcase, Silverman."

"Who the hell are you?" she asked.

A sensation batted at the periphery of Bolan's nervous system. An itch between his shoulder blades turned into an icy breath along his spine. Someone had to be watching them. He peered over the woman's shoulders, seeking an answer. "A friend," he replied as she closed her pistol in the briefcase.

Her voice dripped venom. "My friends don't point guns at me."

"I didn't say I was your friend," Bolan told her. "Get in the car." He glanced back up the street, searching for the unseen eyes. Someone was there, watching for him or the woman.

Silverman didn't move. "You're crazy if you think I'm getting in that car with you. I'd rather take my chances out here on the street. One scream from me, and you won't see anything but blue uniforms on the backs of big cops who're pissed off because they stayed up most of the night for nothing."

Bolan slid the Beretta back under the bomber jacket. He opened the door. "We need to talk."

"We can talk here."

"No, we can't."

"You pulled a gun on me," she said angrily. "How the hell do you expect me to trust you enough to go somewhere with you?"

"I pulled the gun because you would have pulled yours if I hadn't." Bolan tossed the briefcase into the back seat. There. A shadow next to the maroon van. He scanned his memory. How long had the van been there? "And because we don't have time to discuss this on the street."

"How do I know you won't put that gun to my head the minute we leave here and pull the trigger?"

Bolan kept an eye on the van as he moved in closer. He shielded the Beretta from sight and from any attempt the DEA agent might make to take it from him. "I saved your ass earlier. Why would I shoot you now?"

"You also told me your name was Belasko."

Bolan faced her squarely. "Look, Silverman, I'm not here because I want anything from you. I've put most of this thing together already, but I need some confirmation on a few details. I know you and Judson are from New York and

are working on a Canadian operation. I also know you
people have put an undercover agent into the Death's Enforcers. What I need to find out is how badly this operation
is screwed up and if there's anything I can do to help salvage it.''

Silverman slid into the car without another word.

Bolan followed, watching as dark shadows skated across
the undersurface of the van's windshield. The cold itch between his shoulder blades disappeared when he identified
the source. Now if he just knew the who and the why. ''Give
me the keys.''

The woman complied. ''Why can't we talk here?''

Bolan turned the ignition on. ''Because we have com-
pany.'' He dropped the transmission into reverse and eased
out into the sparse morning traffic, switching on the lights
as he did.

From the rearview mirror he saw the van follow suit.
Something bright and hard glimmered behind the vehicle's
windshield.

''The van?'' Silverman asked without turning around.

''Yeah. Do you know it?''

''I noticed it when I passed by.''

''It's been there for over an hour.''

''You say that as if you've been in the neighborhood for
a while, too.''

''I have.''

Bolan worked his way into the thread of traffic, carefully
not losing their pursuers, yet at the same time managing to
create difficult circumstances for the driver of the van to
close the distance if he or she became inclined.

''Somehow,'' Silverman said, ''that doesn't surprise me.''

''That you're being followed?''

''No. That you'd been in the neighborhood. There's an
APB out on you. Did you know that?''

"Yes." Bolan flipped through the mental maps he'd made of this part of Miami, choosing a long, slow route that would take them by Vizcaya, the sixteenth-century-style Italian Renaissance palace that had been built for James Deering between 1914 and 1916. Vizcaya was now the Dade County Art Museum, but the Executioner didn't intend to go that far. The route would allow some privacy while he spoke to the DEA agent and tried to find out who was following her.

"And how do you know the van is following me? You're one of this burgh's hottest mystery men. From what I hear, you don't have a lot of friends in Miami right now. The local chapter of the Outlaws is looking for you. Duncan's business associates would probably like to know who you are. The Miami PD has more than a few questions they'd like answered. And there may be more."

"I don't have a lot of time for chitchat, Silverman."

"Neither do I. Even less time for someone to kidnap me at gunpoint and take me away from my job."

"I want to see if we can come up with some kind of deal."

"No deals." The woman was adamant. "Evidently you've got some knowledge of what I'm working on, but I haven't even got an angle for you."

"That's because I'm working my own angle," Bolan replied. "I was shutting down the cocaine pipeline when I came across your operation."

"That's bullshit, guy. Judson got clearance from every agency working the Miami end of things. We knew all the players, and you aren't one of them."

"Yeah, well, I was an undeclared entry."

"Who are you working for?"

Bolan smiled. "Myself. This pipeline was a private project. I'm not here exactly with blessings from the law enforcement people."

Silverman looked as if she wanted to ask more questions, then shook her head. "Look, I don't give a damn who you're with or what your story is. I'm not going to let you jeopardize the lives of my team."

"Meaning the guy you got undercover with the Death's Enforcers?"

Silverman didn't say anything.

The van seemed content to drift along at a distance, and Bolan let it. "The guy's already in trouble, Silverman. Doesn't it strike you as odd that Duncan only carried enough cocaine aboard the *Swift Tiger* to fill the order for the bikers? Isn't that why your local law enforcement assistance has suddenly gone dry?"

"You don't know what you're talking about."

"Yes, I do. I've been listening to a scanner most of the night. The locals are searching for the Death's Enforcers, and I can figure out for myself that they weren't thrilled with the leftovers you and Judson let them have at the marina. If they find the bikers, there's no telling what will happen to your undercover guy because, officially, he doesn't exist. You and Judson have painted the man into a corner. Unless you go public with the story. In which case you run the risk of getting him killed by the people he's running with."

She didn't respond but sat immobile, and Bolan studied her quietly, sensing the softness of her femininity in the early morning shadows and seeing the troubled emotions tug at her features. He kept the Ford's speed to within the limit, checking to see the van dogging them two car-lengths back.

"You think the *Swift Tiger* was offered up as bait?" the DEA agent asked a few moments later. Her voice had lost some of the hardness.

"Yes."

"But how?"

"I don't know the details, but I think somebody has made your guy and fed the information back to the Miami end that something may have been sour with the deal."

"Then why go through with it?"

"Because it worked. One way or another, there's ten million dollars' worth of cocaine making its way to Toronto tonight. Your operative may be dead by now." Bolan watched his words bite into her, seeing her hands knot into white knuckled fists.

"You could be wrong, you know. Duncan's source may have just set up enough for the buy and not have known who the cocaine was meant for."

"He knew. He named the Corsini Family, but Intel I've managed to get my hands on since then suggests Vincent Corsini."

"Who are you working for, Belasko?" Silverman's voice seemed worn-out.

"Nobody. Like I said, I'm a free agent."

"A wild card." She gave him a bitter smile.

Bolan ignored it. "I came to you because I thought you might want to help salvage this thing before anyone else gets hurt."

"How do you think you can help if the law enforcement people in the immediate area can't find the Death's Enforcers?" She looked at him. "And you're right—there is a special group of vice agents looking for the bikers right now."

"Because I don't think it will end here. I also don't think you and Judson are going to be able to move fast enough from this end to cover your agent's ass when the shit hits the fan. Provided the guy manages to stay alive long enough to get back to Toronto and doesn't get killed or busted along the way."

"You're asking me to trust you with his life."

"I know." Bolan made his voice gentle.

She shook her head slowly. "I can't."

Bolan drifted through the traffic until he reached Collins Avenue, then started working his way back to the police station. "I'm going to leave that briefcase with you when I get out. It has a computer printout in it detailing the Miami pipeline and who the operators were. Check it over if you want, but the names probably won't make any connections for you. Give it to the local vice people. Hopefully they'll find it interesting enough to pull them off the witch-hunt they're working on now."

"This on the level?"

"Yes."

"How did you get it?"

"You don't want to know."

She appeared to consider that. "The vice people will want to know."

"Let them work it out for themselves—it'll take up more of their time. Just tell them it came from me."

"Do I give them a name?"

"No."

"What if they don't believe me?"

"Tell them the biker I took from the Outlaws club is handcuffed and gagged at a boat house in the marina." He gave her the address. "And that they can find Hunsaker dead at his beach house. They'll believe you."

"You killed Hunsaker?"

Bolan nodded. "There's a lot of ragged edges on this one, Silverman, because of the deal your boy cut for Corsini. But the negligible loss Duncan would have suffered at the hands of the vice people leads me to believe you people have an inside man in your operation. Either that or Corsini was in communication with Hunsaker, which is a possibility. Which means if your operative hasn't been compromised and doesn't have dirty hands, he's running for his life right now."

The light from the instrument panel showed the effect his words had on her, underscoring the feelings she tried in vain to keep hidden.

Sudden movement in the rearview mirror drew Bolan's attention. He had just turned off Collins Avenue and was making his way back to the police station and the rental. When he glanced up, he saw the van roaring up on them, the wicked barrel of an automatic rifle poking through the open panel door. He slipped a hand behind Silverman's head and yelled "Down!" as the first bullets ripped into the rear window.

9

Glass imploded from the back window of the Ford and scattered over the seat. Bolan locked the brakes as he reached under his jacket for the Beretta.

The van slid by, autofire still hammering from the open panel door in a bright yellow-and-orange blaze.

The few people on the sidewalks surrounding the street came to a frozen halt. An approaching *Miami Herald* news truck narrowly missed colliding with the passing van as the driver jackknifed the rig to a skidding stop that blocked both lanes.

Rubber burned from the van's tires as the driver fought to regain control of his forward momentum. The rear of the vehicle slewed to one side, then the other, keeping the gunner off balance.

Bolan fought the wheel, releasing the brake as he fed power to the wheels. The Ford threatened to turn sideways for a moment, then fell back into line when he steered into the slide, surging up behind the van.

When the aggressors tried to turn a corner, Bolan cut to the inside and slammed Silverman's car into the van's side, forcing it to swing wide of the turn. Metal shrieked and screeched when the car hit, then crumpled when the van collided with a streetlight. The lamp winked out instantly.

Before the car could finish rocking, the Executioner was on the move, bringing the 93-R to bear as he advanced.

The gunner stood, framed in the warped opening of the panel door on the side, bringing his weapon up.

Bolan removed the man with two 3-round bursts from the 9 mm and ran across the hood of the Ford into the van's interior. The driver was slumped across the steering wheel, his face torn and bloody from impacting against the starred windshield.

Kneeling, Bolan took the man's pulse, finding it thready and weak. He peeled back the eyelids and found mismatched dilations of the pupils, signaling some kind of definite brain injury.

The van rocked as it took on weight.

Bolan glanced over his shoulder and saw Silverman coming through the side door holding her pistol in a Weaver's grip. Her face looked flushed, and tears of blood wept down her jaw from a small cut on her temple. Slipping the Beretta back into his shoulder holster, Bolan asked, "Are you all right?"

"Get your hands up, mister." She held the pistol centered on his chest.

Bolan sighed, halting all movement to look at her. "I don't have time for this, Silverman. In fact, *we* don't have time for it. The Miami PD is going to be here within minutes, and I don't intend to stick around for the head count."

"You're going to stay right here," she said.

Bolan pulled the unconscious driver from the seat and took his wallet. He was aware that the DEA agent's pistol tracked him. He opened the wallet. "This is twice I've saved your life tonight, Silverman. What's it going to take to convince you we're on the same side?"

"A lot more than you've shown me so far. It's not your actions I'm questioning. It's your motivation. You killed Duncan and you say you killed that guy, Hunsaker, in an attempt to close down the cocaine pipeline in the area. That's not my problem. But I do know you might have done the same thing if you're working for another local marketing group intending to take over the area."

The wallet contained almost two hundred dollars in small bills, rental papers for the van and a driver's license. He closed it in disgust, taking in the expensive clothing both men wore. The assault rifle lying across the dead man's chest was an AK-47. Expended shells, scattered across the carpeted interior of the van, gleamed brightly in the light from the dashboard.

"If that was true," Bolan said in answer to her statement, "why would I try to contact you?"

"Because I'm not local talent. You could make contact with me, drop off those papers you say you have and let me make the delivery. If they're good, which they probably are, the vice squad in Miami could finish up the job you started. Then, once I left, you could step out of wherever you'd be hiding and slide right into control."

"Very logical thinking, Silverman," Bolan said. "And just as wrong as it is logical."

Removing the dead man's wallet, he found more cash in small bills and a driver's license and ID. Silverman moved back, keeping her pistol leveled at him. Over her shoulder he could see the crowd that had begun to gather. The only thing missing was the sound of sirens. And he was sure that wouldn't be long. He dropped the wallet on the dead man's chest.

"When the crime unit gets here," Bolan said calmly, "I'd suggest having these two men fingerprinted. Both of them are carrying cash and no credit cards."

"They have ID. I saw you look at it."

"No credit cards," Bolan repeated. "This is a plastic society we're living in now, Silverman. How many people do you know who don't at least have a gas card of some kind? Also, the driver has the rental papers for this van in his wallet. It's filled out to the name on his driver's license, but he paid in cash. Again, no credit card. I figure these two men as out-of-town talent who were lined up for the express purpose of taking you out of the picture.''

"Me?"

"Yeah. I passed them twice before you walked out. They weren't lying in wait for me. It was you they wanted. If they hail from Toronto or other places farther north, I'd say you've got even more evidence that your operation has been compromised.''

"But why me?"

"To protect somebody," Bolan assured her. "You can make book on that. Who it is depends on how badly your investigation was compromised and by who.''

Her face was a study of indecision in the shadows of the van. Bolan could smell the blood and the leaking radiator fluid that became intertwined in the small world they shared and wondered if she was aware of it. For a moment he knew the woman might lean either way. The bore of the 10 mm automatic she fisted never wavered.

"Damn you, Belasko," she said tightly. "Damn you, if I've made the wrong choice." She lowered the S&W's hammer.

"You haven't," he assured her as he passed through the doorway.

"It would make me feel better if I could connect you up with one agency or another."

"I know, but then my security might be as leaky as yours. I learned a long time ago that I operate best and fastest when I'm alone."

"You've been undercover?"

"For a long time."

"Then you know what he's up against."

"The man Judson and you have in with the Enforcers?"

She nodded and leathered the pistol.

"I know."

"I'm going to be dogging your footsteps, Belasko or whatever your name is, and if you cause him to get hurt, I promise you that you'll be able to look over your shoulder one of these days and see me there."

"I believe you." Bolan retreated to the rented Ford and palmed Silverman's DEA badge from her purse, which lay on the floorboard, covering the theft with the recovery of the briefcase. The shield seemed heavy in his pocket when he turned to hand her the briefcase. It wasn't much in the way of official ID but it might be enough to let him pass inspection for a time while he entered the eye of the storm he was tracking. He'd operated on a lot less.

When Silverman took the briefcase, he noticed that none of the indecision was gone from her features.

"It'll work out," he told her, knowing she wouldn't believe him but feeling the need to tell her just the same.

"Yeah, let's hope so."

The sudden keening of a police siren tugged at the frail truce Bolan had declared with the woman, and he could see reconsideration flicker in her eyes. "Take care of yourself," he said. Then he moved back into the shadows as the crowd parted before him. Questions from the onlookers pursued him, but his mind was filled with questions of his own.

Did somebody try to kill Silverman because she was too close to the situation? Because she knew more than she was supposed to? And, if that was the case, was she aware of what she knew?

Bolan didn't think so. His reflection looked gray and two-dimensional in the dark glass of the department store windows lining the sidewalk, then seemed to play hide-and-seek as he moved between street lamps.

Someone had definitely compromised the operation Judson was supervising, and Silverman had, perhaps unwittingly, become dangerous. Who and why still eluded him even in conjecture. What if the undercover agent had turned rogue? That could explain some of it. The man had evidently had his own route figured for getting out of the Miami area, but the puzzle was why hadn't Judson or Silverman known of it? And obviously the DEA team didn't know where the man or the Enforcers were. Otherwise they would be tagging along and not cooling their heels in a Miami police station, waiting to see what went wrong next.

It seemed doubtful that the cocaine or the Enforcers were still anywhere around Miami. But he couldn't leave before he was sure. The trail might be cold, but at least it was still a trail. There might be nothing waiting for him in Toronto if Vincent Corsini was ultimately in control of the events taking place in Miami.

There were a lot of ways to call this one, Bolan realized as he dropped the cowboy hat he'd taken from the Ford into a trash can in the alley he turned into. And maybe a lot of the wrong calls had already been made.

THE CESSNA SHUDDERED in flight.

Rye Thornton glanced at the pilot, feeling his stomach lurch threateningly. "Are you going to make it, Wings?"

The other man gave him a crooked grin that looked forced. "It hurts like hell, bro', but I been through worse and lived to tell about it." He kept one hand on the controls, sucking at a reefer with the other.

Thornton had gotten a small high from passive smoking earlier and still felt twinges of it numbing his mind. But it wasn't enough to deaden the sharp ache of the memories he couldn't remember or the mental uncertainty that told him he wasn't quite sure who he was.

The flight had been long and mostly silent, with breaks only when Wings had sat the Cessna down at the backwoods refueling stops he'd lined up for the return trip. The bullet holes on the side of the plane had drawn attention in

Virginia, Thornton remembered, but the pilot had quickly covered them with a story about a farmer with a shotgun when he'd buzzed a farmhouse outside of Waycross.

He felt his name called from inside his mind. Closed his eyes to the dark sky surrounding them because something out there seemed to fire the dread in his memory. Book covers of King novels he'd read drifted across the scarlet screens on the back of his eyelids. He reached out for them, touched them. Felt touched back. The books. Something about the books. He'd shared them with Alice, enjoyed reading some of the really suspenseful parts of them to her.

Alice.

He dropped the name when he closed a mental fist over it because it burned. Like coals or an acetylene torch. Groped for it when he realized what he'd done, because he didn't want to lose it.

Gone. Only blankness fell into his grasp, blankness and the almost overwhelming guilt.

"Hey, Spider."

Thornton opened his eyes.

"You okay, man?"

Thornton struggled for something to say, having trouble even remembering the words.

"I mean, don't take it personal or nothin', but you sure as hell looked like you vegged out on me a little."

Thornton drew in a deep breath, sucking in the acrid odor of marijuana. "Yeah. Too long on the road, man. And I damn sure could have done without this last shit."

"Yeah."

Shifting in the seat, Thornton peered out the window, trying in vain to wipe off the condensation clouding the glass. It was still night, and even though they were flying at a low altitude, he couldn't recognize any of the landscape whipping by below. His muscles ached from the cramped posture he had to assume, and the shirt Wings had produced before the first refueling stop slid easily against the crusted section of T-shirt clinging to the bullet wound on his side. The pain had dulled, for the most part, leaving only occasional bouts of sharp agony. He guessed the reefer had helped some, but it could have been the pain of the incomplete memories that made the wound pale by comparison. He was sore but he was functional, and maybe even better off physically then he was mentally. The realization scared him, because it brought with it the fear that his control over his mind was slipping.

Inside his head, a voice cautioned. The mind, Sonny, the mind is the keenest weapon you can ever take with you on one of these little outings. But it's up to you to keep it honed. If you don't, it'll work against you at times. Best piece of advice I could give anybody in this line of work.

Thornton struggled to identify the voice. Benny. Benny. Benny something. He was almost certain of it. But he couldn't pinpoint a specific memory, couldn't dredge up an image of the man. And what was the line of work Benny had been referring to?

It didn't have anything to do with his life among the Enforcers—or maybe it had everything to do with it.

Somewhere in there, he had failed somebody. Maybe several somebodies. Was that what he was afraid to face? Was that the force that kept his memory out to lunch?

"Hey. Rye."

The pilot had a concerned expression on his bearded face. He waved a fistful of fingers in front of Thornton's eyes.

"Hey, man. Are you okay?"

Thornton shook his head to clear the confusion away, if only momentarily. "Yeah, yeah. I'm just peachy." He put a hand to his forehead and felt the perspiration on his skin. He felt cold and clammy beneath the clothes. Sick and weak. But it wasn't all because of the wound. "Where are we?"

"Somewhere near Brantford. About ten miles off Lake Erie."

"Get over the lake."

Wings looked confused. "I thought we were goin' on into Toronto."

"We are. Just not in this plane."

"What do you mean?"

Thornton looked at the pilot. "I mean we're going to dump the plane in Lake Erie and find another way into Toronto."

"Hey, wait one damn minute, Spider. This ol' crate may not be much, but she and I go back a ways. She's been more faithful than any woman I ever had in my life."

Thornton put a hard edge in his voice. "She's going to have to be faithful enough to die for you, too, Wings, because we can't show up in Toronto with her."

The pilot put both hands on the yoke. "You didn't say anything about dumpin' her when we set up this little run, Spider."

"I didn't say anything about almost getting put down by Skeeter and Hooter, either."

Wings continued on course stubbornly.

"Hey, man, I'm telling you right now that if we try to slip back into Pearson International or any of the other stops you know along the way, we're going to be drawing the attention of all the torpedoes Corsini will have out looking for us. We don't know what Skeeter told Vinnie about how we were getting back up here. We have to assume he gave Corsini the Cessna." Thornton paused, knowing how stubborn the bikers could be about their possessions. THE BIKERS. Why had he placed himself outside their ranks? Ryan Thornton was captain of the Death's Enforcers, Toronto chapter. And he was riding herd on a ten-million-dollar coke deal that had been totally screwed up. But he was going to walk away a winner, by God. No matter what kinds of memories haunted him. He massaged his temples, aware of the slow headache that had crept up on him.

"It ain't fair, Spider."

"Neither is dying, Wings, and that's surely what we're going to do if we try to take this bird home. Even those country airports you do business with might turn us in for the reward money Corsini will be offering for this shipment. Hell, half of them would probably rather put us down and take the coke and go into business for themselves."

Wings nodded. "Okay, Spider. We do it your way. But I want another plane."

"It'll come right off the top of the profits from this shindig, ace." He felt the Cessna tilt as Wings banked. "Can you fix it so the plane will hit the lake after we jump?"

"Yeah. That won't be a problem. The hard part's gonna be keepin' up with the coke once we start down. Don't want no flares or nothin' to mark the spot."

"If things break our way," Thornton said as he watched the black, ice color of Lake Erie drift into view, "Corsini will believe we went down in the water and our bodies got washed away in the undertow. Along with the coke."

"That'll break his fuckin' heart."

"It should also buy us some time."

Thornton took four parachutes from the rear of the plane and checked them quickly and expertly to make sure they were folded properly. He intended to use the extra one to make a bundle out of the cocaine. He looked up when he was finished and saw the pilot looking at him curiously.

"I didn't know you knew anything about chutes, Spider."

"There's a lot you don't know about me," Thornton said as he started bundling the packs of coke together. He felt his fingers tremble as he knotted the silk lines, trying to remember where he'd learned about packing parachutes. Hell, there was evidently a lot he didn't know about himself.

"GOT SOME ID, BUDDY?" the big deputy asked.

Bolan palmed the DEA badge he'd taken from Piper Silverman's purse and flashed it. In the distance he could still see the ruby glow of receding taillights as a Florida Highway Patrol car moved ahead of him. "Where are the bodies?"

The deputy shifted his chew of tobacco to the other cheek, spit and hooked a thumb over his left shoulder. "'Bout a mile an' a half in. You can't miss it. There'll be this big buncha cops standin' in front of it."

Bolan grinned and put the borrowed badge away. "Got better things to do than keep the press out of the woods, deputy?"

The big man snorted. "Yessir. And better things to do than take you Yankee boys by the hand to make sure no gator don't bite your ass off when you're busy lookin' for clues." He spit again. "You get the notion to go explorin' in them woods, you be careful where you step. Them logs what's got eyes is gators. Be purely too late if you wait till they open their mouth to make sure."

"I'll keep that in mind, deputy."

"You do just that little thing."

Bolan took his foot off the brake and eased the car down the muddy path earlier vehicles had taken. He still wore the bomber jacket and jeans and figured he looked disheveled enough to play the part he'd chosen.

A handful of white disposable cups with coffee stains ringing them jerked and rolled on the floorboard in front of the passenger seat as he bounced over the uneven terrain. He wished he'd opted for a four-wheel-drive unit instead of the car, but it might have stood out too much. Being prepared might have been the motto of the Boy Scouts, but it didn't fit in with the actual way the DEA ran their business. Cost effectiveness said you rented cheap when you were in the field. And 4X4s weren't in that category.

He kept the police scanner under the passenger seat on as he moved toward the crime scene, listening to the deputies' efforts to contain the area and keep reporters away until everything was investigated and filed properly.

A premonition had come over him when he began tracking the reported sightings of the Death's Enforcers, bringing the chill of sudden death. Now, at the site where eight bikers' bodies had been discovered by an early morning fisherman less than an hour ago, he knew the feeling had proved out. One of the things that remained to be seen was whether the DEA undercover agent would be among the death toll.

He guided the rental to a stop under a cypress tree wreathed in Spanish moss and beside a 4X4 Bronco with Sheriff's Department markings on the doors and a light bar across the cab.

The ground felt loose and soft, sinking quickly under the heels of the cowboy boots. The muted conversations from different groups of various law enforcement people didn't penetrate the hush that lay over the swamp.

He came to a halt under a gumbo-limbo tree and watched the three ambulances that were backed to the edge of the swamp water take on the dead. A thin attendant in stained whites finished zipping up a body bag and motioned for another man to help him lift it to an ambulance.

Bolan studied the swamp area. Death was a known component of the primitive Everglades because nature still ruled this section of the swamp with the same iron-fisted doctrine she had handed down a million years ago. But not this kind of death. Not a death that was dictated by killing for pleasure or greed instead of survival.

Pastel fingers of a rosy dawn were just now nudging aside the remnants of twilight but were unable to break the pall that lay over the swamp. Early-morning mist hugged the dark surface of the water, but it would quickly burn off once the temperature started rising.

None of the faces visible to him looked familiar. But that wasn't surprising. His profile had run high on this one, but visual contact had been limited and brief. He didn't worry about people who might notice him now and ask questions later. He could tell from the oil stains floating in rainbow-hued patterns across the surface of the swamp that the game had moved on, making the jaunt to Toronto necessary. Someone had landed a plane on the swamp sometime last night. The lubricating fluid and oil film had come from its engines. And flight was the only fast way out of the swamp. Which was why patrols to the north and along the coast-lines had turned up empty-handed.

The Death's Enforcers had been the couriers for the product initially. But they had died here, at least most of them. So was it a double-cross, or a planned event? Bolan studied the loaded ambulances and twisted the questions over in his mind. Either way, something could have gone wrong. There was still margin for error along whichever course had been charted.

The odds were that the man Judson had insinuated into the operation was lying under one of the stained sheets. But if he wasn't, where was he and whose side was he really on?

And how many sides were involved? The DEA's. Vincent Corsini's. Maybe the undercover agent's. From the looks of things at the swamp, the Death's Enforcers' involvement had been severely cut back.

No matter how he had tried to fit it in, the assassination attempt against Piper Silverman made no sense. She was the undercover's contact with the DEA, but—if that was all she was—how did that make her dangerous to anyone? Or was she playing a side of her own? He had the feeling he wasn't the only one she was withholding information from. And whatever that information or knowledge was, it wasn't an easy burden. He'd seen evidence of that.

He hoped it didn't get her killed when the internal pressure of the operation shattered the loose set of rules overlying it. Turning his jacket collar up against the morning chill, he made his way back to the car, organizing a mental list of the ordnance he'd need once he reached Toronto and wishing he knew more about the parameters of the DEA operation.

10

Rye Thornton popped another penicillin tablet and followed it with a hit of speed. He bent over the water fountain and washed them down, cupping his hand to catch the cold water and rub it over his face briefly. The fever was still burning in him, but it seemed to have leveled off, leaving him weak and lethargic.

He blotted his face on the arm of the fringed leather jacket he wore to conceal the Smith in its shoulder rigging and the .38 S&W Bodyguard he had tucked in his waistband at his back. He didn't feel safe despite the armament. Then realized he probably wouldn't have felt safe carrying a bazooka on his shoulder.

Vincent Corsini was a psychopath, pure and simple. He'd heard it on the streets before ever meeting the man, had seen it in Vinnie's eyes, as well as evidence of the man's handiwork. But where?

The memory shied away quickly, sending a shudder through Thornton's stomach. His eyes rolled, distorting his vision for a moment till he blinked it clear again. He leaned against the concrete wall of the snack area till the dizziness passed, soaking up as much coolness from the surface as he could.

He breathed through his mouth. Blurred visions trampled through his mind, bringing alternating waves of fear and confusion. Memories of the dive from the Cessna, of the wind rushing into his face, of the bone-jarring impact against the ground, of the mad scramble through the forest he and Wings had landed in threaded across his eyelids in a black-and-white panorama that would have done justice to a John Huston film.

"Are you all right, mister?"

Thornton opened his eyes and blinked the speaker into view. She was perhaps six years old, with her raven's-wing dark hair divided into pigtails that trailed down the back of her white dress and a generous smile that revealed the absence of her two front teeth.

"I can get my mom." She placed her chubby hands on the door of the snack area and made as if to go get her mother.

"Wait." Thornton forced himself off the wall and to stand despite the imbalance he felt. He smiled. "I'm okay. Really. I've just got a headache. But thanks for asking."

The little girl looked down shyly, then said, "That's okay." She moved on to the Coke machine.

Thornton left the snack area and drifted back into the main part of the building. He took a few chips from the small bag of Fritos he'd been forcing himself to eat for the last hour, sucking the salt off them before chewing. The salt dried his lips out and made them hurt, but the pain was low-key enough to help keep him alert rather than be distracting.

The wound along his side was tender but it hadn't restricted his movements as much as he'd feared. The doctor he'd taken Wings to had also bandaged him and provided the penicillin. He'd obtained the speed when he'd dipped into a hidden cash reserve to buy the doctor's care and discretion.

He put two more corn chips into his mouth and started sucking, knowing it would make him thirsty again soon but knowing, too, that he couldn't expect the penicillin to stay down on an empty stomach.

He looked around him as he walked, at the science exhibits that invited hands-on participation in the operation

of television studios, musical instruments, electrical storms
and simulated moon-landings. The Ontario Science Centre
was a place he'd been to before. He'd met someone there,
but he couldn't remember who.

He shrugged the thought out of his head. C'mon,
Thornton, get your head back in the situation. You got
control of ten million dollars' worth of Corsini's coke. Half
of this city is going to be gunning for you. The past can't
matter right now. You got the present, good buddy, and that
may not extend past a dozen heartbeats into the future.
You're going to cut a deal if you can, kill Corsini if you
can't, then get the hell out of Canada. Go someplace safe.
Mexico. Yeah. Ain't ever been there.

Or had he?

The thoughts swirled drunkenly inside his head as the
penicillin acted to suppress the infection that fed the fever
and the speed started ripping at the fabric of his mind.

He passed through family groups, fathers showing their
sons and daughters how the different exhibits worked. The
children recoiled from him despite the smile he tried to wear,
and part of him felt sad, felt that something was missing.
The adults put guarding hands on the children till he was
gone.

An exhibit showing the power and fury of thunder-
storms crackled and spit hisses at him, and he found his
hand sliding neatly inside the leather jacket. His fingertips
brushed the butt of the .45 before his brain cataloged the
noises and turned off the self-defense reflexes.

Corsini wouldn't be looking for him here. The Ontario
Science Centre was located at Don Mills Road and Eglin-
ton Avenue, miles from Corsini's residence at the Westin
Harbour Castle. Still, even that knowledge of distance did
nothing to dispel the threat hanging over his life.

But there had been nowhere else to go, nowhere that he
could remember.

He paused at another watercooler and drank till he felt bloated.

Most of the money he'd had hidden away had been spent on the doctor and the purchase of the 4X4 Toyota pickup he had left outside in the parking lot. There wasn't enough left to get far enough away fast enough. Even if he'd want to. There were still debts to pay—for himself, and for Skeeter.

He could almost hear Benny telling him he should have kept more of the money for himself rather than keep passing it on. IF YOU'RE GONNA PLAY THE PART, SONNY, YOU GOTTA PLAY IT FOR REAL. THEY TURN YOU LOOSE OUT THERE WITH A FLIMSY COVER, A GUN, A HEART THUMPIN' THE NATIONAL ANTHEM AND A BELLY FULL OF FEAR. THINK THEY GIVE A SHIT? HELL, NO! YOU GET THE CHANCE, AND BELIEVE ME YOU WILL, YOU LOOK AFTER YOUR OWN SELF. FUCK THEM OTHERS, 'CAUSE THEY'LL FUCK YOU IF THEY GET THE CHANCE. ANOTHER WORLD, SONNY, THAT'S WHAT IT IS. AND YOU GOTTA BE A BIG FISH IF YOU EXPECT TO SURVIVE.

He had nothing else to go by, no face nor a place where the words were said, just the memory of the man's voice. It left Thornton feeling like a cold shell wrapped around the fever.

He halted in the foyer, squinting at the bright late-afternoon sunshine. His stomach made cold, hard knots as he reached for the phone and dialed. A switchboard operator connected him with Vincent Corsini's rooms at the Westin Harbour Castle. A man answered in a low, guttural voice, advising the switchboard operator that Mr. Corsini was in the pool area.

Thornton asked to be connected and waited, listening to the empty buzz of static as the reroutes kicked in. A pool attendant answered, then went in search of Corsini. While he waited, he crushed more corn chips and looked absent-

mindedly at the people coming through the front doors. A
man and his son entered with smiles on their faces, talking
excitedly about the exhibits they wanted to see. He thought
about how nice it would have been to visit the place with
Thad, then had to fight down the urge to throw up. The effort left him weak and dry throated, grasping at the meaning behind the name.

When Corsini came on the line, his voice was tense and
suspicious. "Corsini here. Who's this?"

"I wanted to call you, Vinnie, to let you know myself that
Skeeter missed." Thornton made his words hard, masking
the inner turmoil and questions that still wormed through
him. "I figured you'd know that by now, but I wanted to let
you know I'm still standing, too. I walked away from your
little ambush, man, and I still got your product."

"What do you want, Thornton?"

"I want to know why you had Skeeter try to ice me, Vinnie."

Corsini snorted. "You're a cop, asshole. I knew that from
the minute I laid eyes on you."

Thornton's brain whirled, slinging phantoms of memory
in every direction. Something struggled in the center of that
maelstrom. He went toward it, searching. The pain, the fear
and the self-loathing swarmed over him, taking everything
away but the anxiety. Beads of perspiration trickled down
his face. God, he had to stay away from those feelings. His
hand shook on the telephone. "Fuck you, man. You don't
know what the hell you're talking about. You made a mistake, Vinnie, a big mistake. And it's going to cost you big,
too, because the price on your product just went up."

"I don't need it."

"Fine. I'll burn it. Can you afford to lose ten million
dollars, Vinnie? I mean, everybody knows you ripped a siz-
able stash from your old man before you split with him, but
can you really afford to write off that much this early in
your budding career? Even your old man's pockets have

bottoms, and he doesn't have any more love in his heart for you."

Corsini didn't say anything.

Thornton decided to wait the man out and hung on, grimly saying nothing. In the background he could hear splashing and muffled conversations. His head throbbed with the pain of the fever, and for a moment he thought it had made him deaf.

"What do you want, Thornton?"

He felt some of the inner tension relax. "To make a deal, Corsini. Just like before."

"A deal?"

"Yeah."

"I'm not gonna deal with a cop, Thornton. They lock you up for that shit."

"I don't know where you're getting your information, dude, but it's dead wrong. This is a bad situation we're talking about here. For both of us. You got ten mil invested in the product I can't get rid of. You've got every man working for you and every cop you can buy looking for me and this stuff right now, and I know that. I'm not stupid."

"Let's say for the sake of argument that I'm interested in dealing with you. What kind of arrangement do you want to make?"

"You paid us half the money for the delivery up front, Vinnie. I want it to be like you never paid any at all. You give me the full fee for delivery, and I'll see that you get your product."

"That's..."

"Robbery?" Thornton grinned despite the sick feeling in his head.

Corsini remained silent.

"Yeah, I suppose it is, Vinnie, but let's not fuck around here. Compared to the number you tried to run over me with Skeeter, I'd consider robbery or blackmail a charitable offense under the circumstances. You need this stuff, remember? You got a big deal set up. This'll set you for a lot more deals. At least that's what you told me. Now, provided that you weren't just trying to blow smoke up my ass with how big a man you were going to be after stepping away from your daddy's shadow, you can afford a small setback right now. Dig?''

Corsini hesitated, then said, "I'll give you seventy-five percent of the delivery fee.''

"Wise up, Vinnie. This is a nonnegotiable deal we're talking about. You got all the cards stacked on your side going into this deal. Once you got the product in your hands, I'm open game for every man jack you got payrolled. Don't try to fool me, because I'm no innocent and I'm not going to fool myself. Once I get my hands on that money, I'm going to have to run hard and run fast to even get the chance to spend any of it.''

"That's still a lot of money.''

"Yeah, and it's going to get to be a lot more if I hear you trying to underbid me again. The price is set, Vinnie. Buy in, or I'll close up shop and destroy the stuff.''

Corsini's voice became gravel hard. "I wouldn't do that if I was you, guy, because right now it's the only thing keeping you alive.''

"Wrong. *I'm* the only thing keeping me alive right now.'' Thornton blew out his breath slowly so he wouldn't hyperventilate. The counter woman was watching him curiously. He raked a hand through his sweat-drenched hair and turned away from her.

"It'll take me a little while to get that kind of money together. Tell me where I can get in touch with you when I do.''

"I'll be in touch with you, Vinnie, when I'm ready. You just make sure you're ready, because you're only going to get the one chance to make this train before it pulls out of the station.'' He hung up before the man could say anything else. He left the Science Centre, his heart hammering, urging him to flee while he still had the chance, praying the bad things locked in his mind wouldn't spill out while he still needed his wits about him. Somehow he was more afraid of those unknown thoughts than he was of Vinnie Corsini. At least he could escape from Vinnie.

VINCENT CORSINI SLIPPED back into the cool waters of the pool, trying to submerge his rage as he submerged his body. He wasn't about to be hustled by a fucking two-bit cop with a Clint Eastwood delusion. Thornton wasn't even in a league big enough to try to play hardball with Vincent Corsini. Still, it was a pain in the ass that Thornton had wound up with the cocaine instead of Skeeter.

He swam in short, vicious strokes, the way he'd moved through life since realizing the power he could wield, chopping through the water from one end of the pool and back. He swam underwater the last few yards, burning up oxygen and the anger that wove black spots in front of his eyes. When he surfaced, his lungs were burning. He shook the water from his hair and eyes, gulping in air as he clung to the side of the pool.

His eyes swept across the soft green tile of the poolside checking the faces under the white umbrellas for people who could be dangerous to him. Satisfied, he stuck his arms up and let himself slide back into the chlorinated water. He felt as though he were in slow free-fall as he went under, totally in control.

He liked the way the water bouyed him, supported him, lent its strength to his. Liked the way he could cruise through it like a shark. Yeah, like a fuckin' great white, babe. He grinned, and small bubbles of air escaped through his teeth. Twenty-seven years old and on top of the world.

Almost.

Well, at least he had a toehold on the empire he was planning on building in his near future. Ripped his future right from the dying carcass of his old man.

He kicked out, feeling the power surge within him, glorying in it.

He wouldn't let Thornton get to him. His old man might have to worry about maggots eating into the flesh of the decaying little fiefdom he'd carved out for himself from areas of family business no one else really cared about, but Vincent Corsini wasn't going to worry about no maggots. If he had to, he'd amputate anything that looked infested. Hell, he was young enough to regrow whatever he lost along the way. Young enough, yeah, and mean enough, too.

And that Thornton maggot was going to learn that the hard way.

He broke the surface, took a quick deep breath, then went under again, making a slow, lazy circle before stroking for the end of the pool again.

From the edge of the pool a blonde in a green string bikini smiled at him as she sat slathering suntan lotion on herself.

He raked his lips back, revealing the pearly white gleam that had been one of his first investments when he started controlling his money. The smile and the dream, they'd come together, and his old man had understood neither one. His father had thought the dazzling smile was meant to attract the girls and had been surprised to find that the teeth were only the first installment of the plan to rebuild sixteen-year-old Vincent Corsini.

As Vincent had come to think, Salvatore Corsini only occupied a small fishbowl in what could prove to be a big ocean. And he intended to be a big fish in uncharted waters.

He turned away from the blonde after giving her enough attention to ensure interest at a later time, but not enough to invite her over. He looked at Oscar Gables, a later Vincent Corsini acquisition, and pantomimed drinking and talking on the phone.

The big man stood up, looking as rumpled as usual in the expensive suit—it didn't matter how much money Corsini spent on fittings at the tailors'. Gables stopped at the bar against the wall and came back with a glass and a portable phone.

"Thanks, Oz," Corsini said as he accepted the drink and the phone. He drank the martini and bit into the olive, resisting the impulse to look at the blonde and make chewing a suggestive action. He smiled. Thornton might think he was holding good cards now, but he didn't realize you didn't get good cards when you sat down at the table with Vincent Corsini. A guy might have a chance of breaking even with old Sal on a business deal, but he didn't come close to Vincent the shark.

He poked buttons on the phone, waited for the connection to be made. He didn't know what Thornton hoped to prove by insisting he wasn't an undercover cop. The DEA had planned to stick Thornton into the operation as a hole card, not knowing Corsini had one of his own. Still, Thornton had sounded bad, as if he really meant every word he said and thought he wasn't a cop.

Corsini thought back over conversations he'd had with Miami the past couple of days, thinking that Thornton's behavior fit in with some other things his mind had been working on.

A man answered the phone. "Yeah?"

"It's me. I made contact with Thornton. He says he wants the money, the whole delivery amount, and he'll turn the product over to me. What I want to know is, has Thornton been in contact with you or anybody at the DEA?"

The man was slow to answer, and Corsini knew the guy was taking his time to answer, trying to figure out the angles. "Not with me."

"What about the DEA?"

"No. They'd tell me if he'd made contact with anyone there. He's listed as a rogue agent as of this morning, when all those bikers' bodies turned up in the Everglades."

"What about his girlfriend? Think Thornton's had a chance to chat with her?"

"No."

"Are you sure?"

"As sure as I can be, goddamn it! You didn't exactly keep me posted about the double-cross you had planned at the Miami end. I've been spending some time making sure my ass is covered on this thing."

Corsini laughed derisively. "You're going to worry yourself right out of the money, man."

"What do you mean by that?"

"I mean the money won't do you any good if you have a heart attack now."

"It's not your ass on the line with this thing, Corsini."

"The hell it's not. Who do you figure put up the ten mil at the southern end of this operation in the first place? If this thing goes down the tubes, you lose a skinny pension. I lose a fuckin' fortune. Do you understand that?"

There was silence on the long-distance line.

"I don't intend to lose that product—you understand me?"

"Yeah." The voice was sullen.

"Well, you just keep in mind which side your bread is buttered on. You ride with me, we all go to town in a new Caddy. You try to screw me over or crawfish now, and I send you home in a hearse. Got me?"

"Yes."

"You're going to have to repeat that for me. The line's messed up at this end."

The voice was louder. "Yes, I understand you."

"Good. And now that we got that out of the way, there's one more thing."

"What?"

"I want his girlfriend."

"What?" The voice was almost startled into a yell.

"You heard me just fine. I want Thornton's girlfriend."

"Why?"

"The son of a bitch is trying to play games with me. I intend to up the ante."

"I can't do that."

"Yes, you can. Just remember that if things go to hell in a handbasket, she can testify against you. We're going to have to put them both away. Thornton and the lady cop."

"It was you who tried to have her killed in Miami."

"Yeah. Lucky for me the bozos who tried to do the job muffed it. I wasn't planning on having a use for her after Miami."

"You're asking for too much, Corsini."

Corsini let the anger loose in his voice. "I don't see how you figure that. Hell, I've asked you for precious goddamn little since I come up with this thing. You've sat on your fat ass and waited for the money to come rolling in. Well, we all got to work some time and, buddy, your time is now. Make you a fuckin' star before this is all over."

"What do you want me to do?"

"Just keep her there. I'm sending a couple of guys over to help you take care of it."

"We're supposed to be meeting some people at the RCMP to coordinate the search for Thornton."

"So you'll call and cancel."

"She'll get suspicious."

"So tell her not to."

"It's not that easy."

"It can be if you make it be."

"I—"

"Fuck it, guy. I'm out of choices here. I'm not giving you any, either. Thornton's got my ass up against the wall now. You were supposed to keep that from happening."

"I tried."

"Yeah, well you didn't try hard enough, okay? Now you're going to. You keep her there. Sit on her if you have to."

"I don't understand what Thornton hopes to prove by doing this."

"If you do what I say, Thornton can't prove anything. You just take care of the girl. I'll handle the thinking." Corsini replaced the receiver and signaled for Gables. "I'm through with the phone, Oz, but I'd like another martini."

The big man nodded and scooped the phone up in one massive hand.

Corsini fell backward, sinking into the pool. Water was his environment. No one could touch him there. Invincible. That's how he felt. Despite all the little maggots out there waiting for a piece of him. He surfaced, swimming on his back, noticing the big man in red-striped black sweats for the first time. The man sat on one of the umbrellaed tables, talking on a portable phone, grinning easily as though some babe was talking dirty to him on the other end. Despite the wraparound black sunglasses the man was wearing, Corsini got the impression the guy was staring at him. Trying to find his weak points.

He stared back.

The big man didn't acknowledge the attention.

Corsini let the pool swallow him again, turning his thoughts back to real problems rather than imagined ones. Even if no one else knew what Thornton had on his mind, Corsini figured he did. He smiled as he saw the slender legs of the blonde pass over him, knowing she was letting him know she was more than a little interested. The way Corsini figured it, the DEA's hole card had just gone solo and gone wild.

But, as always, Vincent Corsini was going to hold the winning hand. The queen of hearts, Thornton. Let's see you cover this one.

Corsini smiled again and swam in pursuit of the blonde.

MACK BOLAN CUPPED the mobile phone's receiver to his ear and watched Vincent Corsini talking with the young blonde animatedly. The man was smooth—Bolan had to give him that—with an exterior designed to advertise sensuality to women and confidence to men.

"—guy's a sociopath, Omega," Johnny Tallin was saying. "I don't know of anyone he's ever killed or had killed, but there have been whispers. Things that make the old bosses nervous about this guy. A lot of them, the ones with any sense, are afraid of what Vinnie Corsini might do if he starts building a power base in Toronto. There's been talk of whacking the guy if he steps out of line, because some of the old men are thinking a piece of the New York action might be looking real good to Vinnie about now."

"They also think Corsini could get his hands on New York?"

"Yeah, they do. I've been watching this guy move up. He doesn't take any halfway measures and he's good at organizing things. Hell, Mr. Madrano is getting his kicks watching Vinnie make the Toronto people shake in their boots."

Madrano was Patrizio Madrano, a "retired" Mafia don who lived in upstate New York. Johnny Tallin was Madrano's chief of security. Bolan had met both of them a few months earlier while tracking down information. He had developed a grudging admiration for Tallin, who had proved intelligent, able and willing. They knew Bolan as Omega, a Black Ace of La Commissione, a freewheeler of death in the Mafia houses, who had the power to kill a capo in front of his own soldiers and walk away unscathed.

"I, uh, don't suppose it would do me any good to ask what this is all about," Tallin said.

Bolan smiled, partly because Corsini was watching him again and partly because he knew Tallin knew better than to ask. "You're right, Johnny, it wouldn't."

"That's what I thought. So I won't ask."

"What's Vinnie working on now, Johnny?"

"What makes you so sure I know?"

"You told me yourself Madrano had been keeping an eye on Corsini and, as bodycock for the old man, you'd be the one keeping the focus sharp. You move through Madrano's world, Johnny. You're his legs. I know that."

"I'm not used to dealing information down a one-way street, Omega."

"I know."

Tallin sighed on the other end of the line. "Vinnie's working on a high-dollar dope deal."

"Out of Miami," Bolan said.

"You know about that?"

"I know about it, but I don't know why."

"I got a line on it, but nothing definite. Word on the street is skinny right now. Like I said, Vinnie runs a tight-lipped and organized operation. I've been told he made a purchase of ten mil worth of product from the Colombians by way of a new pipeline operating out of Miami Beach. From what I hear, the guy behind the pipeline is very organized, too."

"Was," Bolan said.

"Was?"

"Was."

"Your information is more current than mine, then, because the last I heard, this guy down south was still in business."

"Maybe it's better in some places, Johnny, but I'm flying blind where Corsini's concerned. What did he need the coke for?"

"He was working a trade with some Swiss arms people. The rumor I turned up was that with the pressure coming down from high-level cooperation between Washington and Bern, trafficking in some areas was getting tight and new sources had to be found."

"So Vinnie wanted to set himself up as a new supplier?"

"Maybe for a while. Vinnie's got a long-range game plan, too—it's just that nobody knows for sure what it is. I figure the guy's got his eyes on some choice spots in Toronto and New York. Areas where it wouldn't take much spilled blood to convince the old guys running those areas it might be easier and safer to move on.''

"Do you think he's capable of that kind of move?"

"Yeah. To be honest, yeah. I'm around these old guys up here a lot, Omega. I don't know what it's like down in your home area, but I get the feeling the days of the big bosses are gone. Legit, hell, even semilegit businesses are paying off in big ways these days. Drugs are still a get-rich-quick payoff for young guys looking to make the grade overnight. But the people who've been around for a while, they know how much computers can know about people and about business and are interested in getting as much computer power as they can. Of course, Mr. Madrano doesn't understand that kind of thinking, but I've been talking to people. You can control a lot of things if you control the right businesses.''

"Like the trucking industry back in Hoffa's day."

"I've heard about that," Tallin said with a chuckle, "but that's not what I'm talking about.''

"You're talking about owning the businesses outright."

"Or owning enough of the blue-chip stock to let the money roll in year after year. A network control of areas like drugs and prostitution is getting to be dead as dinosaurs. At least as far as family business sees it. You got the Crips and the Bloods handling a lot of the crack action, and a don would have to be crazy to take action to the streets to try to control somebody like that.''

"But Vinnie might try."

"For a little while. Long enough to get what he needs out of the situation. Then he's going to move on.''

"What does he want from the Swiss people?"

"They're arms dealers. Black-market types. Switzerland hasn't been involved in any of the world wars, but they've been selling the hell out of arms the past few years.''

Bolan turned the information over in his head, remembering past stories he'd been apprised of through his own Intel as well as what Brognola supplied to him. The black market in Swiss arms had been growing and had caused unrest in that country. As well as death.

"What with the recent American ban against owning any new AR-15s and AK-47s, Vinnie had to go to someone else to stockpile whatever firepower he feels he needs for his coup."

Bolan shifted in the chair under the umbrella. Corsini and the blond swimmer were laughing together over martinis brought by the bodyguard to the edge of the pool. He wasn't used to sitting this long in open territory. He was overdressed in the black sweat suit, but it was preferable to revealing the crisscross of scars across his body.

"Where do the Death's Enforcers fit in, Johnny?"

"I'm not sure, exactly. I've heard they have a road captain named Thornton, who's moved up pretty fast in the organization. Thornton is the one who managed to link the Enforcers to Vinnie's organization through small-time courier service and bodyguard work. Tame stuff compared to what the bikers used to be known for, but sensible, too. Since Thornton took over two or three months ago, the arrest rate for the Enforcers has been down and the money has been up. They can't complain. Hell, maybe Vinnie saw a kindred spirit in Thornton. Also, the word is that Vinnie was going to be able to cover the Enforcers by using the guy he made a connection with in the DEA. I get the feeling that when the time comes, Vinnie will dump those guys, too. They don't fit the corporate image he wants to maintain."

Remembering the sheet-covered bodies he'd seen in southwest Florida, Bolan was sure Corsini had already taken steps to ease the bikers out of his life. He thanked Tallin, listened to the guy make one more pitch to find out what was going on, then hung up.

He replaced the phone inside the briefcase on top of the table, then played everything he'd learned from Tallin back through his mind. A guy inside the DEA? He rubbed the lower part of his face, already feeling stubble returning. Was the hit against Silverman made to take her out because she might know who the double agent in the DEA was? Or was it made by some of Corsini's people who were afraid she was going to back out of whatever deal she might have made with them? It scanned either way. To an extent. But he couldn't assign either motive to Silverman.

She had a secret, yeah, but he didn't think it had its origins in either of those lines of thinking. His gut feeling told him that her trouble lay in another twist of the pattern he hadn't yet discovered.

The straps of the shoulder holster containing the silenced Beretta chafed against bare skin under the warm-up jacket. He fisted the handle of the phone case and moved off, feeling the eyes of Corsini's bodyguard follow him as he walked around the pool.

It was time to loosen up the surveillance he had on Corsini and move out into the field again. If something wasn't happening now, he had to make it happen before Corsini had the chance to bury any signs of the operation he had put together.

But if Silverman wasn't the inside person Corsini had working for the DEA, who was? The man riding with the Death's Enforcers? Or someone else?

11

Piper Silverman stared at her reflection in the hotel room mirror and wished her thoughts could become as tangle-free as her hair, which she was combing.

Too much had happened in Miami. Too many questions had gone unanswered.

And now Ryan was about to be labeled a rogue agent, unless she could figure out some way to get in contact with him and bring him in from the Death's Enforcers and Corsini. Or convince Judson and the DEA that Ryan hadn't gone rogue.

She combed harder, dissatisfied with the way her hair fell and even more dissatisfied with the feeling that her hair was the only problem she could deal with now. Anger swelled within her again when she remembered bits and pieces of the arguments she'd had with Judson that morning. But she hadn't been able to hold her feelings or her fears back after going from ambulance to ambulance, searching for Ryan's body. The undercover operation had taken everything else from Ryan; it couldn't take his life, too.

She had seemed so in control of things at the beginning of the Corsini investigation. So well versed in what to do and what not to do. Yet she'd broken every ground rule laid out for deep work. She'd gotten involved, and she had no one to blame but herself. She couldn't help wondering if Ryan Thornton blamed her, too. God, there had been so much guilt between them. Maybe they'd have been able to set it aside if everything else hadn't happened, too, and if there had been an outside resource for them to go to when Ryan lost his family.

She had seen the loss in him afterward, but they had never been able to talk about it because it would have opened old wounds and made them even deeper. And she had hurt for him, carried her share of the grief and the guilt.

She would have pulled both of them out of the investigation if she could have, even if it meant going over Judson's head. But she knew it would have probably meant losing both their jobs, or, at the very least, demotions. She didn't think Ryan could have withstood that, as well.

Face it, Piper, she told her reflection. Truth to tell, you didn't think you could take the cut, either. You haven't done one totally unselfish thing since you met Ryan. You helped push him in deep, kept monitoring his progress by yourself. He was going to be every bit as much your prize project as he was Judson's. She watched her eyes redden and turned away from the mirror.

She wanted nothing more than to have a good cry. The bath had been good for her as well as necessary. She wiped at her eyes till she recovered control of her emotions. The last thing she needed was for Judson to find her like this. She wished she had been able to sleep on the flight into Toronto the way Judson had. But she had been afraid of the nightmares, afraid that she might talk in her sleep in the way she had when her younger sister used to tease her about it.

She couldn't remember when the last time was that she'd been able to sleep. Even the restless slumber she'd been suffering the last month would have been pleasant.

Slipping out of her robe, she put her undergarments on and dressed in jeans and a loose printed blouse. Judson had said to look like a tourist today because he wasn't sure what they would be doing. It depended on what the DEA and the RCMP researchers could turn up on Ryan.

Rogue.

Judson's term hammered at her.

Rogue.

How many cases had she heard of where deeps actually turned rogue? She had to admit there had been a few. Even more who had been found out to have dirty hands. But Ryan Thornton?

There was no way.

She just wished she could convince Judson of that.

Yet she had to admit also that things looked bad right now. Ryan hadn't made the last meeting with her, hadn't made any kind of communication with any of the DEA task force, and had managed to steal quietly out of Miami in the middle of a manhunt geared for him. Then there were all those bikers' bodies in the Everglades.

Something was definitely wrong with the operation, but she couldn't bring herself to believe Ryan had gone rogue.

She tied her running shoes and was reaching for her shoulder holster when someone knocked at the door. She slid the pistol out, freed the safety and looked out the peephole.

Judson was already raising a knuckled fist to knock again.

She opened the door and stepped back.

"You alone?" Judson asked as he stepped into the room.

"Yes." She held back a scathing remark, knowing it would only have led to another argument. They'd arrived in Toronto less than two hours ago. Who could she have invited into the room?

Judson looked around anyway, trying to mask the movement with his hands as he lighted a cigar.

Silverman put the 10 mm back in the shoulder rig and sat down beside it. "Did something come up?"

"No." Judson shook his head. "Was something supposed to?"

"I know the RCMP have put paper out on Ryan by now.

I thought something might have happened with that.'' *Please don't tell me he's dead.* She didn't know how she would handle that much guilt alone.

"No. Nobody's seen him.''

"Maybe he's not in Toronto.''

"Oh, he's here all right.''

Judson's confident attitude puzzled her. "Has something been turned up?''

Judson squinted his eyes a moment as if to consider the question. He shook his head again. "No, nothing definite. Just a feeling I've got.''

"If it's anything like the one that says Ryan Thornton's turned rogue on this investigation, it's wrong.''

Judson gave her a half smile. "Have you given any thought to what you're going to do if I'm right about this?''

"It would be wasted thought.''

"Would it now? I wonder.'' Judson scratched his chin. His windbreaker fell open, revealing the pistol tucked into his waistband.

Something felt wrong to Silverman, but she couldn't put her finger on it. When had she ever seen Judson tuck a pistol in his pants? The man was usually the last to unleather a weapon in a firefight, and never pulled it till he was sure it was going to be needed.

"A Cessna was dumped into Lake Erie early this morning,'' Judson said. "Luckily it landed near the edge of the lake, where a quick recovery was made by the shore patrol. It had bullet holes in it, Piper, and bullets that matched the ones taken from the bikers' bodies in Florida. Thornton's body wasn't one of those that was found, so we have to assume he was on that plane.''

"But that doesn't make sense, Frank. Ryan would know he was in over his head. He would have known to make contact with someone connected to the operation.''

"That's what everyone else thinks, too.''

"Why wasn't I told about this earlier?''

"I wanted to do some thinking about this before I told you."

Silverman felt her face burn with anger. "What do you mean by that?"

Judson crossed his arms, curling the cigar up in one corner of his mouth. "I mean Thornton seems to have had this caper sewn up pretty good. He's out there somewhere, running free with ten million dollars' worth of cocaine, looking to make the deal of his life."

"You're wrong about that."

"I don't think so. And a lot of the people I've been talking to don't think so, either."

Silverman stood and walked to the end of the bedroom, unable to remain sitting. She folded her arms across her breasts and faced Judson. "Why did you have to think before you told me this, Frank?"

"I wasn't sure how you'd take it."

"If you're going to take me off this investigation, don't you think it would be better to pull me out of the field rather than neuter me informationally and hope I don't get underfoot?"

Judson flicked ashes off his cigar onto the carpet. "Is that what you want?"

"Does it matter what I want? It seems like you're the one making decisions around here by holding out information."

He stabbed the cigar at her, punctuating his words. "Look, missy, I can give it to you either way you want it. You just call the damn tune."

Silverman blinked back her rage, focusing on Ryan and on the fact the man would probably be cut adrift without her. "No."

"No what?"

"No, I don't want to be pulled off now."

"Fine by me," Judson said. "But I want you to know we're going to do this my way. I want our asses covered on this thing."

Silverman forced herself to remain silent.

"I also want to know if Thornton's been in touch with you since we got here."

"We've only been here a couple of hours, Frank." Silverman felt her patience slipping through her fingers.

"That's plenty of time for a phone call."

"There hasn't been one."

Judson sighed.

Silverman felt the wrongness close in around her then, caging her.

"I wish I could believe you, Piper." Judson tugged the pistol free of his waistband.

Not believing her eyes, Silverman watched the barrel swing up in her direction, locking on to her midsection.

"But I don't suppose it really matters any more. If you and Thornton have been plotting something behind my back, it's too late anyway."

Silverman tensed, forcing herself not to glance at the automatic lying on the bed covers. Getting ready.

Judson extended the pistol and said, "Don't, because I'll kill you right here if I have to."

Ducking, Silverman flung herself for the bed, snatching at the holstered 10 mm. She heard Judson curse, caught the man's movement toward her in her peripheral vision, expected to feel a bullet rip into her. Her fingers touched the butt of the pistol, started closing.

A flash of light twinkled to her left, homing in on her temple. Hot pain jolted through her head. Then everything went black.

THORNTON PULLED a New York Yankees ball cap on before stepping out of the pickup in front of the convenience store. The fever had risen again with the approach of nightfall, and the hits of speed operating in his system had thrown handfuls of unrecognizable nightmares at him. Memories, he was sure, that thrust at his consciousness like a videotape hung in fast forward.

Still, the drug kept him functioning despite the fatigue and the sickness of infection raging in his body.

He swept a hand across his forehead as he walked to the public phone in front of the building, feeling the cold and clammy chill that clung to him. He couldn't tell anymore if he was dizzy from the wound or from the speed, or if it was a combination of the two. And he was afraid if he sat down for even a little while, he would stop caring if he took another step.

The clerk behind the counter eyed him with thinly disguised contempt. Some part of his mind, a part that hadn't been walled in by the sections of cognitive thought working toward his survival, didn't blame the man. He felt dirty, knew from his flat, colorless reflection in the store window that he appeared disheveled.

He leaned against the wall, wishing he could soak up some of the stolid strength locked in the bricks. Not much. He didn't need much, just enough to carry him through the next few hours. Then it would all be over. One way or another.

He blotted at his face with the bottom of his T-shirt, using his other hand to make sure the .38 didn't slide from its place at his back. His stomach growled, but he didn't feel the hunger pangs. Speed did that for you.

His hand shook slightly when he fisted the receiver, and he looked at it with bright interest. The shaking subsided, but he wasn't sure if it was because the session passed or because he tried to make his hand remain still. He dropped in a quarter and turned to watch the truck by the curb. It was important, he told himself as the phone rang. The only thing keeping him from certain death was the cocaine hidden up in the spare-tire well under the truck bed. Without it, he'd be trapped here. He needed the money to get away.

"Yeah." Corsini's voice was harsh.

"Me," Thornton said in a soft voice. "Did you get the money together?"

"Yeah. It's chump change, Thornton."

"I know, Vinnie, that's why I gave you the time to get it together." Thornton watched traffic move north on Simcoe from the intersection with Queen Street West. He was closer to Corsini now, and he could feel that registering on him, too.

"I'm a busy man, Thornton. Let's cut the shit and get down to the deal. When and where?"

"There's a record shop on Yonge Street, just south of College, called the Plumrose Passion. Know the one I'm talking about?"

When Corsini said nothing, Thornton forced himself to chuckle dryly. "Yeah, you know the one I'm talking about, Vinnie. You don't have to say a word. I know that record store is just a front for some of your other aspiring business interests. A buyer going to the Plumrose Passion gets his choice of a large range of sixties psychedelic music and designer drugs. I also know the record store is near where you're supposed to meet your Swiss delivery guys."

"You think you've got it all going your way, don't you, cop?"

Thornton looked back at the counter clerk, who turned quickly away when he noticed Ryan maintained eye contact. "I'd say I do. Better than I've had it for a while."

"Don't get used to the good life, Thornton. Everybody's day comes sooner or later."

Thornton grinned. "Vinnie, Vinnie, what are you trying to do? My, my, all this tough talk. What if you actually managed to scare me away? What would you do then? How would you get the coke?"

There was no answer.

"You've got to plan these things out, Vinnie. Once you get things going your way, you don't try to talk the other people involved in the situation into backing out. Donald J. Trump wouldn't be where he is today if he practiced business like that."

"What time?"

"Ten-thirty. Same time as your delivery from the Swiss people. I figure you'll be less inclined to start something stupid if you have an audience of people you want to continue to do business with who'll become disenchanted by dealing with you as the gangster rather than as the entrepreneur."

"I'll be there."

"So will I."

"Make sure the coke is, too," Corsini warned. "The way I see it, this businessman has nothing to lose by making an example of the guy who fucked a deal over for him." Corsini hung up before Thornton could say anything.

Thornton stared at the dead receiver in his hand for a moment, then slowly hung it up. Had the roles reversed while he wasn't looking? Or did it merely seem that way because of the speed? Confidence. Suddenly Corsini was brimming with it, while Thornton's eroded. He checked the clock hanging over the refrigerator section in the convenience store. Two hours till the delivery time, and the record store was less than fifteen minutes away.

His stomach rumbled, growling its displeasure, though he couldn't feel it. He moved into the store, feeling the refrigerated air brush away the clinging fragments of the outside humidity.

He felt the clerk's eyes on him all the way to the cold-drinks section, felt the back of his neck prickle with anticipation. Ignoring the microwavable sandwiches, he reached in and pulled out a quart of orange juice. It wouldn't do to go into tonight's activities with a stomach full of food, a memory told him, because if he was shot in the abdomen, the food could get into his system and fill him with gangrene. Every rookie knew that, and yet every rookie sooner or later got over the fear and started eating during his or her shift again.

Rookie?

He made a frantic grab at the memory, snared it, pulled it expectantly, came face-to-face with a thread that led to Thad and...

His mind reeled away from the sudden impact.

God, he'd almost had something that time.

Feeling the clerk's eyes on him, he moved toward the counter and placed the orange juice on it. He glanced at the security monitor hanging over the area, saw himself and took a minute to study his features. He had a hard time recognizing himself.

Had he looked different?

He was sure he must have. But how?

He stroked the beard, knowing it could easily account for the most dramatic change in the way he appeared. He tried to imagine what he would look like without it.

His momentary self-absorption faded as he became aware that something was wrong.

He locked eyes with the clerk, saw the fear buried in the anxious brown depths of the man's eyes.

The prickling at the base of his neck shot through his system, swinging him dangerously close to taking action. "What's wrong with you?" he asked harshly.

"N-nothing." The clerk stammered twice before he got the word out.

Thornton looked at Simcoe Street, feeling the danger close in. Two boys parked their bicycles to the right of the double doors and came in talking about comic books. The wind rattling through the door gusted across the counter and made a paper taped to the freezer section of the cold-drink tower flutter. He looked at the paper, which was posted so only employees could see it easily, and noticed the official markings.

He placed his palms on the counter and leaned across, and the clerk leaned back, raising his hands in self-defense.

The black-and-white reproduction was grainy, caused partly by the retake and partly by the copying, but he could tell the man on the paper wore his face. He made out Ryan Thornton, Dangerous, Toronto Police Department, and Immediately. Then the wind gusted again and blew it out of sight. He looked back at the clerk as the fear built up inside of him.

He took the .38 from his waistband and pointed it at the clerk. The man had taken note of him and had seen the pickup. Maybe the clerk had called the police already. Thornton's finger curled around the trigger, holding the pistol straight out, pointing at the man's head through his hands. He willed himself to pull the trigger, wanting to break a link in the chain that tied him to this store, to this now. He needed to be lost. Only for a couple more hours.

"No, please don't shoot," the clerk said the closed eyes.

Thornton felt the pressure in his arm—like an overfilled balloon winding the length of his arm—wanting to explode. He willed himself to pull the trigger, giving the intent greater action. He couldn't allow the man to live, to interfere with his plans. If he didn't kill the clerk, it would be like committing suicide when he went out on the streets. And the streets held his only chance of escape.

The two boys had frozen, staring at him in openmouthed awe.

Thad. As Thornton's mind registered the presence again, the name came into his mind, and with it, another influence.

Thornton's hand shook. "Down on the floor, old man," he said through gritted teeth.

The clerk lay on his stomach, still protecting his head with his hands.

Thornton moved around the counter, keeping the .38 leveled before him. He ripped the paper from the drink tower and scanned it. There was no information about why he was wanted, but it did carry a tag line about his being armed and dangerous. Something twisted inside his mind, as if part of him couldn't believe it was his face he saw there. Not his. He wouldn't believe he could become one of the many he had seen during his years. He wadded the paper up and dropped it to the floor, forcing himself to think, to act. There was no question the photograph was of him, wearing a face he seemed to be more comfortable with than the one he had now. He tried to remember when the picture had been taken. He'd been arrested before, but the picture didn't look like it had been cribbed from police records. It looked like it had been obtained from an employee file of some sort. He'd seen enough of those in his time, too hadn't he? But where?

Still moving, he ducked under the counter and ripped out the phone. If the clerk hadn't already called the police, he could at least delay the call after he left.

Back on the other side of the counter, he fisted the orange juice and lifted the .38 up. He fired two shots, filling the store with shock waves of explosions and turning the monitor into twisted, shattered wreckage that barely hung from the support struts.

Then he was through the door, racing for the pickup, pausing only long enough to rip the pay phone out. He hit the ignition after throwing the .38 and the orange juice onto the seat. Shifting into reverse, he backed out onto Simcoe Street, hoping the clerk wouldn't see his license number.

His heart was pounding as he navigated the late-evening traffic. He brushed perspiration out of his eyes as he constantly checked his rearview and side mirrors. Armed and dangerous. Running for his goddamn life. Running from Corsini, from the Toronto cops, from whatever kept rattling around so uneasily in his head. He clenched his fists

around the steering wheel, watching the lights spin crazily
in the periphery of his vision, willing the waiting to be over
and knowing it would be over too soon.

BOLAN TRAILED in Corsini's wake, maintaining enough
distance so as not to arouse attention yet staying close
enough to keep his target in sight. He'd picked the man and
his group up on the first floor in front of the elevators while
mixing with the group of people attending a function in one
of the hotel's banquet rooms. He wore a dark turtleneck and
a charcoal-gray suit that looked carefully cared for and allowed him to merge effectively with the banquet crowd while
maintaining surveillance over the bank of elevators. But a
practiced eye could have seen the cut of the coat was a bit
long, a bit too generous at the lapels so it would cover the
hardware he was carrying.

But Corsini's men had the only practiced eyes in the area
and they were intent on getting their boss through the
crowded lobby to the parking garage. There were four of
them, running a basic two-two pattern around Corsini.

Bolan clung to the outside of the lobby, smoothly and
unobtrusively ducking, dodging and apologizing in polite
undertones when necessary. Corsini's movement could
mean only one thing: that the cocaine had surfaced somewhere and was on the move.

He could feel the fatigue drop away from him as he tailed
Corsini, knowing his body was automatically sliding into the
battle high that could carry him for hours more yet demand a tremendous payback when the time came. He knew
when a warrior started dealing with the devil in the hellzones, it was usually with his own body, pushing it beyond
its limits in the name of flag or cause or country. Not just
staying alive. A goal like that was too thin to cast a shadow
across the killgrounds that were a warrior's home. To live
as a larger-than-life person in a battle zone, a warrior had

to face a larger-than-life task. Survival was just taking care of the equipment.

Finding the DEA's undercover agent in the mess of double-dealing that had arrived in Toronto would be harder than finding a needle in a haystack. And he had to keep that needle alive if at all possible, while everything else went up in a chain reaction.

Corsini and his crew passed through the door leading to the adjacent parking area. When the last man paused to look back over his shoulder, Bolan became one of a small group talking around an ashtray, fitting an appropriately disarming smile on his face. The minute the guard had satisfied himself that no one was taking undue interest in Corsini and had passed through the door, the Executioner followed.

He unbuttoned the jacket as he passed out into the parking garage, giving him instant access to either the 93-R or the heavier Desert Eagle. Numbers were falling. He could feel them. Corsini had seemed too self-assured, too ready for whatever had been set up.

Yet if everything was going precisely as Corsini would have it, would the man show up anywhere around the cocaine? Bolan didn't think so. So far there was no legal evidence that could connect the drug shipment to the man. So it seemed unlikely that Corsini would voluntarily take the risk, unless he didn't have a choice and unless he was sure the DEA and the RCMP were going to be out of the way for the exchange.

But if Thornton was the undercover cop, wouldn't he have called the DEA in for the exchange?

Questions continued to assault Bolan's analytical mind, twisting and turning till he was sure there was no mental footing to even begin knowing what was going on. Nothing to base a strategy on. Only the immediacy of it was a certainty.

The parking garage was well lighted in the center, trailing off to deeper shadows along the perimeters he stuck to. He paused behind a thick concrete support when Corsini came to a halt in the center of the open area. One of the men separated from the group.

Bolan kept moving, angling for the Jeep Cherokee he'd rented once he arrived at Toronto.

Another car entered from the street, coasting to a stop in front of Corsini.

Bolan shifted, coming closer to the group, hunkering down so his shadow wouldn't stand out against the car he was using for cover. A light came on in the dark sedan as the driver gestured to someone in the back seat. Bolan recognized the man as somebody who'd been around Corsini's room earlier. Then he recognized Piper Silverman in the back seat nearest him.

Was she Corsini's inside connection with the law enforcement people? Bolan the man didn't want to think that way; Bolan the warrior had to take in every consideration, even the distasteful ones. And right now it was the warrior side of him that would keep him alive. He waited.

Corsini leaned forward and said something through the open rear window. Silverman spit on him, struggling in a way that let Bolan know the woman had her hands cuffed behind her. A knot of apprehension he hadn't noticed dissolved in his belly. He'd made mistakes in judging people before, but not many. And he'd have hated to have been wrong about the gutsy lady.

In response to the spitting, Corsini shook a handkerchief out of his pocket and wiped the spittle away. Then, still smiling, he reached inside the car and slapped the woman, rocking her head back.

Bolan duck-walked closer, the .44 Magnum already in his hand, waiting for the opportunity. Acting too soon would cost Silverman her life. He felt himself tense and forced himself to relax, the numbers still falling softly all around him. He could still reach out and make them his own, shift the pattern to where everything reacted from him instead of to him. It was all in deciding the right moment to act.

Pausing at the front of the station wagon parked near the open space of the parking area, he listened.

"Give me five minutes," Corsini was telling the driver, "then start after me. Stay out of the immediate area until I call you. Got that?"

Corsini then leaned forward and pointed across the driver's seat. "You're coming with me."

Frank Judson climbed out on the other side as Corsini's car came to a halt behind him.

The picture started to come together in Bolan's mind as he examined the possibilities implied by Judson's presence. If Judson was Corsini's man inside the DEA, it cleared up a lot of things, except for where the undercover agent fit in.

Corsini and Judson climbed into the back of the dark blue Cadillac with the driver and another man. The remaining two followed in a late-model Chevy.

The sedan with Silverman and the two men rolled forward, making a large circle.

Bolan stepped away from the station wagon as the sedan came around to face him, holding the Desert Eagle behind his leg, eyes burning as he tried to stare through the bright headlights and smoke-tinted windshield. He knew it was going to go down fast and only hoped he could keep Silverman clear of the heat. She was obviously an important facet of whatever plan Corsini had in mind, so her captors wouldn't want to harm her. At least not yet.

He was still forty feet away when the sedan faced him head-on. As he brought the .44 up into target acquisition, framing the driver's side, he heard the engine suddenly roar and the tires squeal as they surged forward.

Standing his ground while the heavy car bore down on him, he placed four shots through the driver's side, knowing there wouldn't be enough power left in the powerful projectiles to bore through the man's body and the seat—they wouldn't be a danger to Silverman.

Then the car was on him, and there was no time to run.

12

Piper Silverman recognized Belasko only a heartbeat before she saw the big pistol come up in the man's hand. Twisting instinctively, she fell across the seat, waiting for the sound of shots. The windshield shattered inward. She saw the spiderwebbed chunks of safety glass fly toward the back of the car. She flinched, then watched the view afforded by the gap between the bucket seats as the big man's shadow rolled over the hood of the sedan.

She waited for the sound of that impact, too. But it didn't come. Then the shadow was gone as quickly as it came, leaving a broken and splintered panorama visible to her. The driver's arm dropped lifelessly between the seats.

Unguided, the car floated out of control and smashed into a concrete pillar.

She was thrown forward to collide with the back of the seat before being bounced back where she started. A coppery salt taste tainted her tongue as the lump on her temple threatened to explode her into unconsciousness again. She groaned, the sound barely audible above the roaring of the car's engine.

"Who is that son of a bitch?" the man beside her growled.

Silverman ignored him, trying to find a position that wouldn't bring pain to her cuffed wrists. Her hands and fingers felt slick, and she was sure she was bleeding from at least one of her arms.

Her guard shifted, dragging a mammoth revolver from a shoulder holster. It was a Smith & Wesson .357 with an eight-inch barrel, and even in her precarious situation she couldn't help thinking that the hardguy had a definite need to impress.

Silverman kicked her feet against the door, wanting to see if the impact had loosened the lock. Her feet pounded against it futilely, drawing her captor's attention at once.

He pointed the .357 at her face, and she stopped moving.

"Georgie!" the guard yelled. "Hey, Georgie!"

With an arthritic shiver, the engine died and silence filled the interior of the car.

"Georgie!" The guard reached forward, then jerked his blood-covered hand back instantly and gagged. He looked at her with fear-filled eyes. "He's dead! Georgie's dead! He ain't got no face."

Silverman wondered where Belasko had gone to. She couldn't believe the big man had sacrificed himself on a half-baked rescue attempt. Belasko had seemed to be a man with all the right moves; he couldn't have gone down under the car.

"Out of the car, bitch," her guard said, glancing apprehensively over his shoulder out the rear window. He looked back at her, noticing she hadn't moved. "I said get out of the car, bitch."

Silverman forced her voice to remain calm. "I can't get out by myself," she said. "I'm handcuffed, remember? I'm going to need some help."

The guard grabbed her by the links holding the handcuffs together, bringing her arms up between her shoulders and creating excruciating agony.

"Do you know who that son of a bitch was?"

"No." Silverman got to her knees, slipping and sliding across the car seat as the man dragged her out.

"The car hit him, didn't it?"

She bit back a cry of pain, reached down tentatively with her foot to establish her balance and hoped he wouldn't spill her facefirst across the concrete. The temple hurt bad enough by itself. "I think so."

"Me, too. Only now I don't see no body."

Both feet on the ground now, Silverman turned to look back the way the sedan had come, searching for Belasko.

"C'mon, bitch," the guard said, "tell me who that big bastard was and be damn quick about it."

"I don't know."

Yanking her around, the guard locked an arm over her shoulders and across her breasts and pressed the muzzle of the .357 deep into her neck. "I don't believe you. That son of a bitch was after you. Me an' Georgie, we didn't know him. That leaves you."

Silverman's eyes swept over the parked cars, searching, painfully aware of the gun pressing into her bruised flesh. "I don't know him."

"Yeah, sure." The guard squeezed her breast hard, making her yelp despite her best efforts not to give him the satisfaction. "Hey, man!" the guard yelled over her shoulder. "I got this bitch you want so bad. See? And if you don't show yourself by the time I count to three, I'm gonna take her head off. Then it'll be just you an' me."

Silverman swallowed hard, trying to divorce herself from the events, trying hard to find a shred of sanity and sense to cling to. "Maybe that's the way he wants it," she said in a calm voice. "Maybe he just wants it to be you and him."

"Shut up!" The guard shook her, putting pressure on her windpipe. "That what you want, man? You want me to kill this bitch?"

Silverman saw the shadow come out of the darkness twenty feet away, moving from concealment behind a van. The big pistol was held at his side, pointing down. She felt her insides ice over as he approached.

"Drop the piece, man," the guard ordered.

Belasko shook his head, a grim look on his face.

Silverman tried to look through the piercing blue of his eyes, tried to get an idea of what thoughts were cycling through his brain. But there was nothing she could see.

"I said drop the piece," the guard repeated.

Belasko shook his head. He took another step forward.

"I'll kill her, man, I swear I will."

Belasko smiled, a chilly and grim smile. Silverman thought the effort would have looked more at home on a shark's mouth. Don't give up the gun, she wanted to shriek, knowing that if Belasko did, they were both dead.

"What would Vinnie say if he found out you killed the woman you were supposed to be guarding?" Belasko asked.

When the guard didn't say anything, Belasko took another step forward. The .357 pressed harder against Silverman's neck.

"Think Vinnie would just let it slide?" Belasko taunted. "Or do you think he'd kill you?" His lips curled back again tautly. "Personally I think he'd put a bullet in your head and drop you in a lake."

With a cry of inarticulate rage, the guard took his weapon from Silverman's neck and pointed it toward Belasko.

She caught a glimpse of movement as Belasko shifted, saw the muzzle-flash that exploded suddenly in his hand, and waited for the bullet to smack into her flesh, knowing he couldn't hit the man without hitting her first. Her eyes closed involuntarily, then she felt the guard yanked backward.

With the breath caught in her throat, she turned to look at the dead man sprawled on the concrete behind her with the top of his head taken off.

"Who has the key to the cuffs?" Belasko asked as he checked her for injury.

"Him." She pointed to the dead man.

Still holding the big pistol, he checked the body and found the key. He released her from the cuffs and urged her toward a parked Jeep Cherokee.

"Hold it right there, mister," a warning voice called, "and put the gun on the floor."

Silverman looked around to see a gray-haired security guard pointing a four-inch .38 at them.

"It's okay, guy," Belasko said as he extended his hands upward and smiled easily.

Silverman watched him display a badge in his left palm, feeling better that the man had been with some agency after all, that it might help in explaining the Judson situation. Then she recognized the badge as her own. She struggled to keep her mouth shut, realizing that if she called Belasko's bluff, they'd be stuck for at last an hour trying to get it all sorted out. By then it would be too late to help Ryan.

"I'm an American drug enforcement agent operating through the RCMP," Belasko said, "and I'm pursuing the other part of the team these two men are with. I need you to call the Toronto PD and get somebody down here to seal off this area. I don't have much time. Tell them we may need a bomb squad, too."

"Bomb squad?"

"Maybe," Belasko said as he lowered his hands and tucked the badge and gun away. "We should know more in just a few minutes. Now, get a move on it."

The security guard leathered his gun, saying, "Yes, sir," then reached for the walkie-talkie on his hip.

Belasko helped her into the Jeep. "Are you okay?"

She nodded, still amazed at how quickly he had taken control of the situation. Just as he had back at the Miami marina. Yet he fit the mold as a man of action, someone others would turn to for leadership instinctively. "A few bruises, but nothing that's going to keep me from going with you after Corsini."

Belasko flashed a quick smile, and she thought it odd that at such a strange time and under such strange circumstances she should find that she liked the smile.

He got in on the other side and drove toward the entrance.

"That's my badge you have."

He handed it back to her without a word.

She felt it cold and hard and heavy in her hand, made even heavier by the promises she'd made when the DEA had first given it to her and by the compromises she'd made since then.

Belasko pulled out on the street. "Do you know where Corsini is going?"

She nodded. "A record shop called the Plumrose Passion."

"Is Thornton going to be there?"

"Yes."

"What's the address?"

She gave it to him, bracing herself as he drove.

"I know Judson's on Corsini's payroll," Belasko said as he shifted on the fly into four-wheel-drive and powered the Jeep onto a sidewalk to get around vehicles waiting for a traffic light, "but I need to know the rest of it, too."

A sick, cold knot formed in Silverman's stomach, fighting against the adrenaline letdown from the events in the parking garage. God, where to begin? She wished she didn't have to tell him, but knew she had no choice. For Ryan's sake. Belasko, unknown but not unproven quality that he was, seemed to be her only ally.

She took a deep breath and launched into the story.

VINCENT CORSINI LEANED forward and said, "Do a drive-by, Tommy, and let's see if we can spot any friends Thornton might have brought along for this little shindig."

The driver nodded as he made the gentle turn onto Yonge Street off College.

Corsini looked out the windows, scrutinizing both sides of the street, taking in the neon lights advertising books and records and XXX-rated features. He didn't like doing business in that location, even though the Plumrose Passion was a successful enterprise. It made him feel dirty. But maybe that was just a result of the upbringing his father had given him. You are better than other people, his old man would tell him, clapping him on the back in a manly way while scraping nickels and dimes together from other places just like this area. Father and son, working the same areas for the same kind of illegal business, except for the drugs Corsini had introduced to the street people or taken over from those who were involved in private enterprise. And the other difference was the fact that Corsini planned to let his career begin here, in these dirty streets, then use it as a stepping-stone to propel himself to heights his father had never dreamed of.

"You're wasting time," Judson said. "Thornton's gone rogue. He's operating independently."

"I hear you, Frank, but for all you know, you may be getting suckered, too."

Judson appeared to be uncomfortable with the idea. He turned away and looked out the window.

"If I remember correctly, you told me this operation would be a piece of cake a month ago. In fact, it was your idea to use Thornton on the drug buy in Miami. Great coverage, you assured me. Transportation guaranteed by the DEA because everyone thought Thornton was getting close to a big bust against the growing Corsini empire. You even painted me as a big fish to some of your supervisors so they'd let you have a free hand in Florida. Now I have to go out on the streets looking for a property that should have been in my hands by now."

"What happened back in Florida to all those bikers?" Judson demanded. "I may have sold Thornton to the DEA as the guy who pulled the trigger, but I don't buy that myself.''

"That was insurance," Corsini said, unruffled.

"Bullshit," Judson said. "You went off half-cocked and got the shaft for your trouble. If you hadn't pulled that play, maybe Thornton would have already dropped into our laps by now."

"And maybe he would have been even farther away than he is now, Frank."

Judson had nothing to say to that.

"I didn't have as much trust in your boy as you obviously do. You say he's rogue—I say the fact of the matter remains to be seen."

"He didn't tell Silverman anything about this," Judson replied, "and she seemed surprised as hell to learn that I was working with you."

"Maybe I should be wondering if you are," Corsini said with a thin smile.

"Bullshit, Vincent. I got too much invested in you to help sink you now."

"And I have too much on you," Corsini agreed. He pulled out the Sig-Sauer P-226 leathered under his arm and made sure the chamber was filled, then rested it on his thigh. He noticed Judson's eyes widen at the appearance of the pistol. "Partners in crime, Frank, that's what we are."

Corsini turned his attention to the driver. "What did you see, Tommy?"

"Looked good to me, Vincent. Maybe a handful of customers inside the place."

"What about the perimeters?"

"I'd know an unmarked car if I saw it," Tommy assured him. "There weren't any there."

Corsini lifted the car phone and dialed. "Okay, Carmine, talk to me."

"Alleys are clean, Vincent. We've cruised them twice and only turned up street trash."

"Good man, Carmine. Now get ready to sweep that trash. We'll be going inside in fifteen minutes." He hung up. "Tommy?"

"Yo."

"Let's make the meet and see if the Swiss guys showed up with the artillery." Corsini sat back, watching the street filled with neon signs flash by, feeling his pulse rate increase with the coming confrontation, knowing there was no way he was going to allow Thornton to walk away from this. And maybe not Frank Judson, either.

"RYAN THORNTON WAS the deep selected to penetrate Death's Enforcers," Silverman said. "He had a lot going for him—he was good with motorcycles, knew the counterculture, had worked drugs before, knew the kind of business he'd be dealing with. What he didn't plan on was having to stay deep for eight months."

Bolan listened as he drove, hearing the pain that underscored the words. He couldn't help but wonder, with the intensity of emotion that was involved, if he would get the whole story.

"Originally Thornton was on semiloan to the RCMP from the DEA to bust the bikers for deals being conducted between Toronto and New York. Drugs, white slavery, insurance fraud, the usual gamut you can expect from the biker gangs. Then everything assumed a larger scope when Vincent Corsini started using the Enforcers for little things that quickly grew into larger things."

"Like a ten-million-dollar shipment of cocaine from Miami."

She glanced up at him, skin looking milk pale in the silvery moonlight, the pent-up frustration and inner turmoil inscribing taut lines around her mouth. "Yes."

"I saw Judson with Corsini," Bolan said as he negotiated a turn on Adelaide Street East. "Where does he figure in this?"

"The agency put him in charge of what suddenly became the Vincent Corsini operation."

"There were no rumors about Judson's link with Corsini?"

"As far as I know, there never was a link until this case."

"Is Thornton in on this?"

She looked away from him and he knew he'd hit a nerve.

"Piper," he said gently, "the time for bullshit and hesitation is gone. If you haven't noticed, it's only you and me now. There won't be any backup for us. I need to know what's going on." He watched tears fill her eyes.

"I don't know anymore, Belasko. Really, I don't. This whole thing is my fault."

"Tell me about Thornton."

"Ryan's a good cop. A good man. They shouldn't have kept him deep for so long. I started noticing him slipping away a couple months ago, but I didn't say anything."

"What do you mean you noticed him slipping away?"

"He was in too deep for too long. He was beginning to identify with the bikers, was beginning to think of himself as belonging more to them than to the DEA. He didn't want to keep gathering evidence against them. Just Corsini. He became especially close to a member named Skeeter Davis. Do you know what I mean?"

"Yeah. A type of codependency. I've seen it on the battlefield and in relationships that have developed between terrorists and their hostages."

She banged her fist on the console. "What you don't understand is that I was supposed to be his safety, his anchor to the reality that was his real life. Not the one he was playing. I fucked everything up."

"How?"

She bit her lip as he watched and knew she was forcing herself to go on. "Ryan was having trouble with his marriage. When you're deep, it isn't easy to get home on a regular basis. And he was uneasy about the relationships he'd had to develop with the bikers' women. Casual sex in the line of duty is one thing for a single man, but not for someone who's married. And to play the part, he had to live the part. Things began to come apart at home. Alice, Ryan's wife, wanted him home. He couldn't turn away from the assignment, because he believed in what he was doing. He turned to me for help. Instead, I gave in to emotional feelings of my own. I was weak when I should have been strong." Her voice broke and seemed to freeze.

"You had an affair?" Bolan asked, trying to sound soothing.

She nodded.

"It happens, Piper. You and Thornton were sharing a world that had no one else in it. It's hard to escape that kind of reality when no one else even admits it exists."

"What do you know about it?"

"I've seen it happen. I've been there. Over half my life has been spent on one battlefield or another, Piper. You learn to take life when and where you can, between heartbeats, because that's the only refuge you have when you can't lay the battle down." Old memories twisted through Bolan's mind, beginning with the girls and women he'd known in Vietnam, shifting to Val Querente, Toby Ranger, moving on to others he'd known and loved in the hours allotted to them during his wars. Luckily his war had kept him moving, leaving him no time for regrets. He was glad none of those relationships had been as messy psychologically as Silverman's and Thornton's. But then, in his life, he never had time to consider the future, any future, the way Silverman and Thornton had. Nor time enough to judge his past.

"We tried to stop ourselves," she said. "Honestly, we did. But it seemed like the more we tried not to, the sweeter what we shared became. And Ryan's movement up in the Enforcers and the ties to Corsini started taking up more time, making it harder for us to be together." She swallowed with effort. "A month ago Ryan and Alice had a fight, and she said she was going to leave him. He didn't know what to do. The night he left to return to Toronto, Alice's car was hit by a tractor-trailer in upstate New York. She and Thad were killed instantly.''

''Thad?''

''His son. He was nine years old.''

Bolan experienced a wave of empathy for the undercover agent and quickly made himself shelve it—an emotion like that had no business going with him into the hellzone he was headed for.

''Judson gave orders that Ryan wasn't to be pulled out of the field till everything seemed safe. The higher-ups agreed because doing so might have caused Ryan's death. He never got to attend the funerals, and I had to tell him. I tried to get Judson to, but he refused, saying I was the contact officer and it was my duty. So Ryan had to hear it from me, the woman he'd been committing adultery with.'' She paused. ''Needless to say, after that it was hard to speak with each other. But I felt him slipping, and I couldn't do a damn thing about it except go over Judson's head.''

''But you didn't.''

''No. I knew it might result in getting us both fired or demoted. I don't think Ryan could have handled that on top of everything else. See, his work means a lot to him. He lives and breathes and believes in what he does. He's a damn good man, Belasko, despite everything else that has happened to him.''

Bolan didn't try to dissuade the challenging light in the woman's eyes. ''So where to do you think Thornton stands now?''

''I think he's lost himself.''

''What do you mean?''

''I think he's submerged his real identity under the deep cover. I think he believes he really is Ryan Thornton, road captain of Death's Enforcers, Toronto chapter. I think he's using the deep to hide from everything that has happened to him.''

"What leads you to that conclusion?"

"The things I've seen. The things I heard Judson say earlier. Corsini was going to use me as a bartering chip to get the cocaine from Ryan."

"Thornton has the cocaine?"

"Yes."

Bolan kicked it around in his mind as he made the left onto Yonge Street, checking street numbers. It was a ten-million-dollar jackpot on the table with Corsini, the DEA and him sitting in.

And Ryan Thornton was the wild card in the deck.

"He's got to be running, Belasko. He's scared, hurt, confused, and he's running for his life."

"Why hasn't he turned to the DEA for help?"

"That's what convinced me he's submerged himself in the deep. With everything else that's happened to him, he would have checked in with somebody. He's convinced himself he has nowhere to turn."

"What happened back in the Everglades?"

"From the way the locals pieced it together, it was a double-cross. Two bikers operated the Uzis that killed the rest of the members, only to be killed by a .45. Ryan carries a .45. One of those bikers believed to be in on the double-cross was Skeeter Davis."

"Leaving Thornton no one to trust."

"Yes."

"Is Thornton salvageable?" Bolan watched her try to squirm away from the question.

"I want to say yes, Belasko, because I want to believe it. I screwed Ryan's life up. I don't want to be the reason he loses it. But I don't know how far under he is. He's living and running on animal instinct now, hurting and not knowing why. With the proper help and time, I think he can be."

Bolan nodded. "I'll buy that." He pulled off Yonge Street and found an alley that led to the rear of the Plumrose Passion a few blocks away. He cut the lights and coasted, watching the rooftops, marking the distance mentally. He stopped the Cherokee about a block and a half away from the record shop.

"I might be wrong," Silverman said. "I have to tell you that because I don't want to lie to you or to myself. Not anymore. I don't want that on my head, too."

Bolan looked at her, looked at the swelling on her temple that partially closed her eye. "You've got a lot of recovery to go through yourself, Piper, and you don't have time for a damn bit of it before this thing goes down. Until the situation is contained, you're going to be a cop. A damn good cop, or you're not going to be any good to anyone and may help get all of us killed. Do you read me?"

She leaned her head back against the seat and nodded.

"Afterward you'll have to pick up the pieces as best as you can. Thornton will need help there, too. Provided we get him back. You've both got a lot to get over, and you can help each other as long as you're willing. You put yourself down now, fault yourself for doing one thing you consider wrong, and you may blow whatever chance we have to patch things up."

"I need a gun," she said. "Judson took mine."

Bolan handed her the Beretta. "Have you seen one of these?"

She inspected it professionally. "Beretta. 93-R. I'm familiar with it."

He showed her the settings. "Single shot. Three-round burst. Use whatever the situation calls for, but remember we've got civilian activity in this area, too." He gave her a half-dozen extra clips, then reached into the back of the Cherokee for the Uzi and the bags of ordnance he had ready for the assault.

Outside the vehicle, he stripped out of the suit to the blacksuit he had on underneath. He hung the ordnance around his waist from military webbing, then pulled on a trench coat over it. He gave Silverman the bomber jacket, knowing it wouldn't draw much attention in the neighborhood they had just entered.

"Keep the pistol in your hand under the jacket," he advised, "because when this goes down, it's going to go down fast."

She nodded. "You look like we're heading into a war zone."

"Make no mistakes about it," Bolan said as he started toward the building. "We are."

VINCENT CORSINI DIALED the number again, still getting a busy signal. He was annoyed. Georgie should have answered by now. The phone shouldn't have been off the hook. He looked back at the front of the Plumrose Passion, knowing something had somehow gone terribly wrong.

Suddenly his whole future seemed to be hanging on this deal tonight. He dialed Carmine's number again and tapped his fingers nervously on the hood of the Cadillac until it was answered. "Something's gone sour," he said in a controlled voice. "Georgie's not answering his car phone. I want you to get some guys inside that record shop and shake Thornton out of it. If you have to do it publicly, do it. You and the other boys can take a nice long vacation stateside afterward. Just make sure you earn it." He replaced the phone in the car and stared down Yonge Street, wondering what secrets the neon lights hid.

He glanced back at the Heimdall Freight Lines truck that was parked around the corner on Gerrard Street East. The two Swiss soldiers delivering the goods sat motionlessly in the cab. They were bookends, both with overdeveloped bodies and long, stringy blond hair hanging to their shoulders. Rudolf and Edouard, he'd been told. No last names.

They'd also volunteered the information that they weren't willing to wait long.

Corsini paced tensely, aware that every minute that passed could allow things to get that much worse.

And when it came, the sudden sound of gunfire almost stopped his heart.

THORNTON MOVED through the Plumrose Passion carefully, feeling the press of time. Scattered all around him were racks of albums, 8-tracks and posters of rock-and-roll singers from the 1960s and early 1970s.

The clerk behind the counter wore purple-tinted octagon-shaped glasses, love beads and a leather vest over a lavender T-shirt. He looked easily old enough to have lived during the Make Love—Not War generation as an adult.

It wasn't easy being surrounded by so many things from the past. They all called out to him, offering memories if he would only look closer, perhaps touch an album cover, even listen on the earphones provided at the end of the middle rack.

He shut himself off from them, willing the memories away. He had enough to do without getting lost in the thunderous roll of yesterdays that threatened to suck him in. He concentrated on the hard lines of the .45 under the fringed leather jacket. This was his reality. The threat of sudden death.

"Something I can help you with, man?" the clerk asked.

Thornton shook his head. "Just looking."

"It's cool, jack, just trying to be helpful."

Thornton turned away from the man and started to flip through a stack of LPs without seeing any of the titles.

Then the back door exploded inward. Two men carrying shotguns stepped inside, aiming at his waist. "Touch the piece, asshole, and you're history," one of them said.

Thornton dived to the ground, raking the .45 from its leather, grunting painfully when his wound hit the floor.

There was a sudden boom, then the top of the stack of albums he'd been looking at turned into streamers of confetti.

He rolled, getting to his feet, using his free hand to help him scramble across the floor toward the door. More gunfire tracked him, smashing into the walls and shredding posters.

Then he was out the door and face-to-face with a memory that brought all the nightmares tumbling into bright focus. Piper. Piper was here. He reached for her, confused, not knowing what was real and what wasn't. He saw the gun in her hand, and tears in her eyes and heard his name on her lips.

Then a subsonic whoosh rushed by his ear, and the bullet hit her high in the chest and knocked her away from him.

He looked at her, lying unmoving on the sidewalk, and felt the scream well up in him from far way. "Nnnnooooo!" He wheeled, bringing the .45 up in a two-handed grip, spraying fire at the man across the street who was already firing again. He felt something bite into his flesh, on the same side as the earlier wound but refused to go down.

BOLAN STRODE through the darkness in silence, keeping the Uzi tucked under the trench coat. Silverman had gone around the front, leaving the back door for him. A sedan wheeled into the alley with its lights out, cruising to a stop behind the record shop as he took refuge behind a corner one building down.

Two men with shotguns got out of the sedan, making no effort at all to conceal them. One of them raised his weapon to his shoulder and fired, blowing the lock off the door, then kicked it open before the sound of the shot faded from the alley.

The Executioner was in motion at once, whipping the Uzi out as he ran for the back door. He'd given brief consideration to the possibility that the men were Toronto cops, but their actions ruled that out.

He closed in on them unseen, getting a brief glimpse of the carnage they were wreaking inside the shop even as he swung into action. He slammed the fold-out stock of the Uzi into the neck of one, sending him crumpling to the ground and the shotgun sliding across the floor.

The other shotgunner tried to turn, whipping the sawed-off barrel of his weapon around.

Bolan blocked the shotgun with the Uzi, sweeping the man's feet out from under him with a leg, then kneeling quickly as he went down to knock him out with the submachine gun. The shooter relaxed instantly.

More firing came from outside on the street.

Bolan moved through the tattered racks of albums and 8-tracks and cassette tapes, ignoring the clerk, who was holding his empty hands out. He looked through the plate glass window and saw Ryan Thornton firing round after round across the street just as the window collapsed into jagged shards of glass that rained down onto the tiled floor.

Thornton staggered, and Bolan knew the man had taken at least one bullet. Instead of retreating or trying to find cover, Thornton stood his ground in a wide-legged shooter's stance, his weapon still spitting death.

Bolan thudded into place behind the concrete section of the wall framing the door and the gaping space of the empty window. He ducked around the corner, spraying the 32-round box of the Uzi dry at the gunners across the street, sending them fleeing for cover. Then he reached forward and grabbed Thornton by his leather jacket and pulled him down. Bolan rammed another clip into the Uzi and glanced up in time to see two men trying to cross the street as the others provided covering fire.

Slithering across the broken glass of the window, Bolan came up suddenly, the Uzi's stock tucked neatly into his shoulder. He touched off two 3-round bursts that stripped coordination from each man and left them lying like discarded heaps in the middle of the street. An oncoming car swerved to miss the bodies, then sped away.

Bolan looked back at Thornton, seeing the blood spreading down his side. The undercover man had the .45 aimed at the Executioner. "How bad is it?" Bolan asked.

"Who are you?" Thornton demanded, grimacing with the pain. He tried to stand up, but his foot slipped on the pooling blood and he went back down.

"Mike Belasko," Bolan replied. "I'm the guy that just saved your ass."

Thornton seemed to consider that for a moment, then let the .45 drop across his thigh. "They got Piper," he said lifelessly.

Bolan pushed his feelings away, forcing himself to stay locked in the military mode. He raked a blast of fire across the street, dispersing the gunners again as the 9 mm rounds pummeled the brick facing of the building behind them. "Where is she?"

"Outside." Thornton's eyes inside the dark hollows looked dead and empty. He made another attempt to get up and managed to pull himself unsteadily erect.

Bolan ignored the man for the moment, feeding another clip into the submachine gun. It wouldn't be long before the Toronto police arrived on the scene, even with the bomb scare he'd dropped as a diversion on the security guard at Corsini's hotel. The action here was too hot to hold.

He hazarded a glance around the corner, looking for Silverman, saw nothing but a smear of blood on the sidewalk. "She's not there."

"She gotta be," Thornton insisted. "I saw her go down." He started to go past Bolan, but the Executioner held him back just as a handful of bullets from the gunners exploded wooden splinters from the door frame. He forced the man against the wall, feeling the numbers spill out of his control, knowing he's never really had a chance to contain the situation once it hit the streets. He felt bad about Silverman and hoped she was all right. At least she was still on the move.

"Where is the cocaine?" Bolan asked as he stripped out of the trench coat.

Thornton dropped the magazine out of his .45 and checked the rounds, then switched magazines, placing the half-empty one in a back pants pocket. He looked at Bolan and said, "Thad's dead. Alice is, too."

"I know, Ryan," Bolan said softly, realizing the man was hovering between realities, between the firefight taking place here and now and the nightmares he'd been avoiding for weeks. He'd seen men slip into shock in Vietnam and knew it took time to come out of it—time he and Thornton couldn't afford. "I need to know where Corsini is."

Thornton spoke in a whisper. "Down at Gerrard Street. That was the plan. He was going to make the trade with the Swiss munitions people there." He swallowed with effort. "The bastard double-crossed me. Talked Skeeter and Hooter into trying to kill me. The dumb sons of bitches. They should have known he was lying to them." He chuckled. "Hell, I should have known he was lying to me. But I didn't, did I? I got them killed, got Alice and Thad killed, got Piper killed." He winked at Bolan. "You might be better off shooting me yourself, pard, before I get you killed, too."

"I've got to go after Corsini," Bolan said. "That leaves you to look for Silverman. Are you up to it?"

"She's dead."

"No, she isn't. But she's hurt pretty bad, judging from the blood. She might not make it without help."

"She went down so goddamn quick. I thought she was dead."

"She's alive." Bolan wanted the man to focus on the thought, hoping it would be enough to keep him going.

Thornton fisted the .45 and nodded. "I'll find her."

Bolan gave him a quick smile. "Way to go. When you do, there's a Jeep Cherokee parked in the alley. The keys are on the floorboard. Use the car phone to let the Toronto PD know there are undercover officers on the field. Got it?"

"Got it."

Bolan plucked a grenade from the harness he wore. "When this goes off, run like hell and don't look back."

Stepping around the corner, Bolan tossed the grenade in an easy underhand throw that sent it skittering up under the sedan most of Corsini's men were hiding behind. He ducked back inside as bullets chipped at the entrance, commencing a silent countdown.

The grenade erupted, splashing orange-and-yellow lights across the doorway.

"Go!" he yelled to Thornton, spinning around the corner to offer covering fire.

Thornton sprinted for the back door, favoring his wounded side.

Flames spilled from the destroyed sedan sitting on its side, sending bright-colored talons scratching for the night-dark sky. Silhouettes, some of them on fire, scattered from the sedan.

Bolan took the fight to the street, charging into the hell-zone, hoping that Thornton could carry through long enough to find Silverman and that she was going to be okay.

Two gunners went down immediately under the Uzi's withering line of fire, dropping to their knees and falling forward. Then he squeezed off mercy bursts that took care of the burning shadows and silenced the screams of agony.

Bolan crossed the street, circling around the burning wreckage of the car, securing the area before moving on, feeling the press of time push him mercilessly. He rammed a fresh magazine up the pistol grip of the Uzi and pounded down the sidewalk, seeing frightened faces peering at him from the windows and doors of the shops he passed.

Bullets streaked toward him from a gunner hiding in the alley between the buildings, pounding sparks and stone splinters from the sidewalk.

The Executioner wheeled, changing direction, dropping into a roll as he stretched the Uzi out before him, seeking the man. He triggered a long burst, sweeping it across the gunner's position as he rolled, coming to a stop on his elbows and firing a final burst that ripped the man from the wall and spilled him like a stringless puppet in the alley.

Then he was up again, running, watching the mouth of Gerrard Street as a truck bearing the name Heimdall Freight Lines roared onto Yonge. His lungs burning from the exertion, he forced his body to break into full stride, closing the gap between himself and the truck, swinging the Uzi by its strap over his back. The truck rumbled with effort, its transmission straining to pick up speed, then clanking as the gears changed. The chain-covered tarp beat at the back door soundlessly, the noise lost in the grinding of the engine.

Bolan stretched, gaining on the freight truck, his legs aching with the effort, the boots feeling too heavy to lift another step. Finally he reached, curled his fingers in the chain, felt himself pulled off stride as the truck shifted into a higher gear. He hoisted himself, tucking his body against the truck, feeling the agony shift from his legs to his arms, willing himself to hold the grip. The only chance he had of shutting everything down was here. Now. He gritted his teeth against the pain as his body beat against the truck.

Corsini's Cadillac whipped around the corner of Gerrard Street, its headlights splashing against his legs. He saw a muzzle-flash come from the passenger side of the luxury car, followed by a handful of others. Then the truck started swaying from side to side, letting him know the driver was aware he'd clambered onto the truck. Bolan tried to lift himself higher, then felt something burn along his leg. He missed his handhold and went swinging wildly away from the truck.

MEMORIES WASHED over Thornton as he stood in the alley-way. God, he wanted away from them so desperately. His .45 felt like a lead weight at the end of his arm, dragging him down into a torrent of immobilizing guilt.

He forced himself to think about Piper despite the pain her memory brought. She was out here somewhere, needing him.

He pushed away from the back of the record shop, stumbling in the darkness, never sure how far away the ground was. Every time he took a step, his legs seemed to spring back up at him, moving independently.

As he passed an alley, strong arms reached out to seize him, knocking the gun out of his hand as they pulled him close. He felt fetid breath burn along his cheek, felt the metal flange of a gun sight prod under his chin.

"Don't move, Thornton," Frank Judson's voice whispered hoarsely in his ear, "or I'll take your goddamn head off." The arm around Thornton's neck tightened, shutting off his wind.

"You understand me, cowboy?"

Thornton nodded weakly.

"I want the cocaine, Thornton. You and Silverman and that big bastard in black have cost me everything else. I was damn lucky Vinnie didn't shoot me, but he was too interested in getting the guns from the Swiss people to stop when I jumped out of the car."

Thornton coughed.

Judson screwed the flange of the gun sight into his chin tighter, bringing increased pain.

"You were with Corsini?"

Judson chuckled as he shoved Thornton forward. "Gee, you're a regular whiz for a burnout, aren't you?" He pushed again. "Now, let's go get that cocaine and, if you're lucky, I'll put you out of your misery."

SILVERMAN PRESSED A HAND over the wound in her shoulder, feeling blood ooze over it immediately. She listened to the gunfire and squealing tires coming from the street. The last thing she remembered was seeing Ryan, seeing the confusion on his face, seeing the hollowness that seemed to cling to him like a second skin.

She struggled to her feet, vaguely remembering pulling herself back into the alley, sure Ryan would have followed her. There was nowhere else for him to go. The record shop was full of shooting men, too.

Where was he? Had he been shot?

Her left arm dangled uselessly at her side, numb from the shoulder down. She bent over to pick up the pistol Belasko had given her, feeling the blood coating her fingertips stick to it. The effort almost sent her to her knees. She fought the sickness, willing herself not to black out again. There was too much to be done.

She forced her head to clear and listened to the shooting vanish down the street, then heard voices coming from the alley in back of the Plumrose Passion. Voices she recognized.

Ryan's.

And someone else's.

Using the wall, she made her way back to the alley, elbowing her way down while keeping the Beretta up.

Slivers of moonlight fell across the two men when she peered around the corner. She saw Judson standing behind Ryan, holding a gun at his throat, then memory of the voice clicked into place, as well. Warm blood continued to soak into her blouse under the jacket.

She stepped out into the alley, pointing the pistol at Judson's back less than fifteen feet away. She tried to steady her hand, blinked her eyes in an effort to clear them, hardened her voice and said, "Put the gun down, Frank."

"Is that you, Piper?" the man asked, freezing in place.

"Yes. I'll shoot if you make me, Frank."

"Will you, now? Somehow I don't think you will, Piper, because before you get the chance, I'll blow your boy-friend's head off." Judson twisted his head, shifting slightly with Ryan. "See, Piper, I don't have anything left to lose. In fact, killing me would probably be better than putting me in prison. A faster death, for sure. You know what they do to cops in there."

Silverman's arm trembled with the continued strain of holding the Beretta up. She wanted to shoot. God, she wanted to shoot. But she wasn't Belasko or Annie Oakley. The alley was dark, she was in bad shape, Ryan was too close and she couldn't remember if the pistol was on single-shot or 3-round burst. Peering over the sight, she watched Judson turn around completely, placing Ryan between them.

"Put the gun down, Piper," Judson said, "and I won't kill him. I just want the cocaine and I'll take my chances with getting out of here before the police come."

She kept the pistol leveled.

"Don't do it, Piper," Ryan pleaded.

"Drop it," Judson ordered, thumbing back the hammer on his pistol.

"Shoot the son of a bitch, Piper!" Ryan screamed.

Silverman let the Beretta fall from her fingertips. "I can't."

Grinning, Judson removed the pistol from Ryan's neck and pointed it at Silverman. She didn't have the strength to evade the approaching bullet.

BOLAN FLOATED OUT away from the truck, holding on to the chain with one hand, swung by the rocky momentum. He flailed like a bass, managing to get his other hand back on the chain net just before he surged back into the back door with enough force to drive the wind from his lungs. He twisted, gasping for breath, wrapped in the chain net and the tarp for a moment, managing to hook a foot in the chain squares before swinging outward again.

The gunner in the Cadillac continued to fire quick shots that were burning closer as the luxury car closed the distance.

Bolan was barely able to pull his lower body out of the way as the Cadillac's driver hit the accelerator and rammed the back of the truck. The truck shivered from the impact, skating wildly across the street as the driver overcontrolled it.

Car horns blared in indignation. There was the sound of a muffled impact from the front, then Bolan saw a passenger car go out of control and slam through the plate glass front of a café.

He swung out again, scrabbling for the Uzi, finding it, brining it up waist high.

The shooter in the Cadillac was leaning out of the car now.

Bolan squeezed the trigger of the Uzi as he swung back toward the truck, cutting a swath of 9 mm tumblers across the windshield of the luxury car, taking out the shooter. The body tumbled from the window as the Cadillac swerved out of control and fell back.

Taking advantage of the next outward swing, Bolan checked where the truck driver was heading and saw the end of Yonge Street approaching. He knew the massive vehicle could never make the sharp turn at the end of it with the kind of speed it had built up.

The transmission whined, sending shudders through the truck, then powered up again as the big wheels left the street and plowed across the grassy area leading to Queen's Quay East.

Bolan slammed into the back of the truck, feeling the chain mesh bite into his hand, wondering if he had broken any fingers. Something crashed, and he saw boards scattered in their wake as the truck plowed through one of the seasonal vendor's stands that fronted the public area of Lake Ontario. Then he realized the Swiss team must have been heading for the Island Rent-a-Plane on Lakeshore Boulevard.

The driver bore his theory out when he continued west.

Using his other foot, Bolan pushed himself out to the left side of the truck, switching hands, as well. The Uzi in his left hand now, he leaned around the side of the truck, his chest banging hard against the rear of the vehicle. He scrambled farther down, till he could see the tires, and waited, knowing he had to take the truck out now before any more lives were endangered.

When the driver started to turn the big tractor-trailer around, trying to head the vehicle back to Lakeshore Boulevard, the Executioner squeezed the Uzi's trigger, taking out all the tires on the left side in one sweep. Already off balance from the momentum, the truck fell outward, veering across the sidewalk that separated the road from Lake Ontario.

Bolan let himself go, floating with centrifugal force, tucking himself in as he spun toward the black water.

THORNTON MOVED before Judson could fire, ramming an elbow into his midsection, then smashing a right into the man's face as he spun free. The gun went off with a loud report, deafening his left ear.

Thornton kicked out, connecting with Judson's wrist and sending the weapon spinning.

Judson hit him with a backhanded swing, screaming out in rage. Another blow threatened to cave in Thornton's ribs, and he tried to cover up, only to be smashed in the mouth. He tasted the blood as he fell back but forced himself to scramble to his feet, remembering Piper. He hit Judson with a body-slam as the man was reaching down for the pistol.

They went down together, lost in a desperate tangle of arms and legs. Thornton tried to pummel the man, working himself into a frenzy of blows, surprised at how much he really wanted to live. Then a hard right fist knocked him off Judson.

His head fuzzed over, and he lost his balance, falling twice before he could even get to his knees. When he did, he saw Judson swinging the pistol toward him, but the next moment Judson's head came apart in bloody sections and his body folded like a rag doll's.

Breathing in ragged gasps, Thornton looked over his shoulder.

Piper stood there, holding her pistol out, then letting it drop to her side as she ran toward him.

He made himself stand and caught her when she reached him, staggering under their combined weight and lost in the tears they shared.

"Are you all right?" he asked, stroking her hair back, not noticing he was leaving bloody streaks until it was too late.

"No," she said. "Are you?"

Somewhere inside all the pain and the guilt, he found a smile for her, and he was even more surprised by its presence than by his will to live. "No." He still cringed inwardly from all the memories her presence turned loose, yet he was grateful, too, that those memories were his again. He hugged her fiercely, closing his eyes as he reached out for Alice and Thad, finding them there. God, it hurt. But hurting was better than being empty the way he had been these past few weeks. To lose the memories, the love—that would have truly been a loss.

"Ryan?"

"I'm okay," he said, knowing it wasn't true. Not yet. Maybe not ever completely okay again, but better.

Sirens pealed over the street sounds and the sporadic gunfire to the south.

"Where's Belasko?" Piper asked, but Thornton shook his head negatively.

When she pushed him toward the Cherokee, he paused long enough to pick up Judson's gun.

BOLAN HIT THE WATER and lost the Uzi somewhere along the way, then was buffeted by another shock wave as the front of the tractor-trailer hit the lake. It wasn't deep there, hardly more than chest high, but it took him a moment to get his bearings. He stroked for the surface, aiming for the moon. He sucked in a lungful of air, shaking the water out of his eyes.

Sirens screamed across the lake surface, sounding hollow and distant.

Something skipped along the water in front of Bolan, followed immediately by the sound of gunfire. A muzzle-flash flamed in the periphery of his vision just as something dug leaden fingers into his shoulder. He went over backward with the force, sinking under the water as he drew the Desert Eagle. His arm came alive with the pain of movement as he swam under the lake surface.

Bullets searched for him, leaving silver-stained streamers curling after them when they hit the water. He traced the muzzle-flashes, coming up suddenly with the big .44 framed in target acquisition.

A blond man with stringy hair tried to wheel toward him.

Bolan pumped two rounds from the Desert Eagle, scoring on the man's throat and the middle of his face as the muzzle climbed. The blond man was blown over backward, crumpling into a disjointed heap that hung into the water.

Wading forward, aware that the sirens were closing the distance, the Executioner checked out the interior of the truck, finding another blond man hanging halfway out the broken windshield. Blood and diesel fuel and oil covered the lake surface, curling out from the wreck in ever-widening circles.

Satisfied no one else was in the vehicle, he made his way to the rear of the truck, sitting just on the edge of the sidewalk, five feet above the water. The catch on the sliding door had broken, and crates containing assault rifles had spilled out.

Bolan reached down and hefted one. It was a Swiss-made Sturmgewehr 90 chambered for 5.56 X 45 mm ammunition. It was a deadly piece in the right hands and a good choice for Corsini, since IVI Dominion Industries in Canada made the ammunition.

Car brakes squeaked to a halt nearby, and headlights sprayed over the edge of the pier.

Unhurried, Bolan knelt and reached into a shattered box of ammo, coming out with a 100-round bandolier, sectioned in ten 10-round strippers, and slipped the magazine out of the assault rifle. Using two of the strippers, he quickly loaded the magazine and charged the weapon. He left the buttstock folded, fisting the pistol grip and gripping the folded bipod built onto the front.

"Find him! Spread out and find that son of a bitch!"

Bolan recognized Corsini's voice even over the keening police sirens. He slid into the inky shadows clinging to the broken pier, moving to come up on the other side.

"Vincent," another man said, "we need to be thinking about getting the hell out of here. The cops will arrive any minute."

"You'll get out of here when I say you'll get out of here, Tommy," Corsini said. "I want the son of a bitch who did this. Now, get out there and find him."

Bolan stepped into view, tracking onto the two men flanking Corsini as they moved along the water's edge. His first 3-round burst took out the man on Corsini's right. The next burst took out the man on the left, ending the rapid line of autofire that raked across the concrete toward Bolan's feet.

Corsini was in full flight, racing for the battered Cadillac. Just as his hand rested on the door handle, Bolan opened up, tearing a jagged line of bullet holes that closed in on Corsini's hand, chasing it from the door.

The rifle fired dry and Bolan tossed it away. "Your call, Vinnie," he said calmly.

"Fuck you, cop," Corsini said as he locked his hands behind his head. "Go ahead and arrest me. You don't have a damn thing on me that's going to keep me locked up for long. What do you have? A burned-out cop whose track record isn't going to be exactly a picture of health after everything is exposed in the courts. You can't hang the cocaine on me—I don't have it, your pal the narc does—if he's still alive. And the arms deal—who's going to testify against me? You didn't leave any of them alive." Corsini smiled, obviously enjoying his seeming triumph in the middle of disaster. "Face it, cop, you don't have a case. Who's going to find me guilty with all this circumstantial evidence?"

"Me," the Executioner replied as he drew the .44 and removed Corsini's cocky smile for good.

Take
4 explosive books
plus a
mystery bonus
FREE

Do you know a real hero?

At Gold Eagle Books we know that heroes are not just fictional. Everyday someone somewhere is performing a selfless task, risking his or her own life without expectation of reward.

Gold Eagle would like to recognize America's local heroes by publishing their stories. If you know a true to life hero (that person might even be you) we'd like to hear about him or her. In 150-200 words tell us about a heroic deed you witnessed or experienced. Once a month, we'll select a local hero and award him or her with national recognition by printing his or her story on the inside back cover of THE EXECUTIONER series, and the ABLE TEAM, PHOENIX FORCE and/or VIETNAM: GROUND ZERO series.

Send your name, address, zip or postal code, along with your story of 150-200 words (and a photograph of the hero if possible), and mail to:

LOCAL HEROES AWARD
Gold Eagle Books
225 Duncan Mill Road
Don Mills, Ontario
M3B 3K9
Canada

The following rules apply: All stories and photographs submitted to Gold Eagle Books, published or not, become the property of Gold Eagle and cannot be returned. Submissions are subject to verification by local media before publication can occur. Not all stories will be published and photographs may or may not be used. Gold Eagle reserves the right to reprint an earlier LOCAL HEROES AWARD in the event that a verified hero cannot be found. Permission by the featured hero must be granted in writing to Gold Eagle Books prior to publication. Submit entries by December 31, 1990.

HERO-1R